Separated

Dear Phillip,

Before I opened my eyes this morning, I asked for words about you. I got *change, home, sad.* I guess you've left your receiving home and have gone to your foster one. I don't blame you for feeling sad. It makes me feel bad that I get to stay with our aunt and you get farmed out. It's cruel to separate brother and sister orphans, especially twins. But at least we have some ways of reaching each other . . .

point

DOUBLE TROUBLE

**Barthe DeClements &
Christopher Greimes**

SCHOLASTIC INC.
New York Toronto London Auckland Sydney

ISBN 0-590-41248-5

12 11 10 9 8 7 6 5   0 1 2 3/9

Printed in the U.S.A.   01

First Scholastic printing, April 1988

This book is for my lovely daughter, Mari, who blazed the trail ahead of me. B.D.

There are unlimited ways of viewing the world . . . or worlds.

These pages have been written in honor of all pioneers who are opening roads to the realms within. C.G.

DOUBLE TROUBLE

January 15

Dear Phillip,

I felt you in my room last night. It was comforting to have you there, and I wanted to tell you my wrist hurt where Mr. Gessert wrenched it, but I knew you couldn't answer. I soothed myself into sleep by deciding I'd write you as soon as I woke up.

Before I opened my eyes this morning, I asked for words about you. I got *change, home, sad.* I guess you've left your receiving home and have gone to your foster one. I don't blame you for feeling sad. It makes me feel bad that I get to stay with our aunt and you get farmed out. It's cruel to separate brother and sister orphans, especially

3

twins. But at least we have some ways of reaching each other.

What was bothering me last night was Mr. Gessert. He's the big topic in ninth grade. All the kids want to be in his social studies room instead of in boring Mrs. Fenwick's. With Gessert, we either have a class discussion after reading our textbooks or we listen to his fantastic stories. He made us practically itch with lice and our gums bleed with scurvy when he told us about the Spanish sailing to the New World.

The kids would like to call him Bill, but since you're not supposed to call teachers by their first name, they compromise and call him Mr. G. The younger guys find sticks with crooked tops to flash around like he flashes his cane. I did think his cane was neat, silver handle and all. I thought he was OK, too, until yesterday.

Yesterday after school, Sue Ellen and I were selling our band candy—or at least that's what I thought we were doing. It was freezing when we started out. The third house we went to had a thermometer stuck on a pole in the yard and it said 23°. I had the hood of my jacket pulled over my head and my wool gloves on, but it was my feet in my Nikes that were cold.

After going to thirteen houses and selling nine bars, four of mine, five of Sue Ellen's, I suggested we circle back around Lake Stevens Mall. (Not a mall like the ones nearer Seattle, this is just a country one—a grocery store, a bank, a library, and a post office.)

Sue Ellen said no, no, we had to get the candy sold fast

before the other kids covered the area. It made sense, so I plodded along with her, wishing I had boots on like she did. Between houses, Sue Ellen asked me what boy I liked in junior high. I said I thought Jake Krakowski seemed interesting.

"Oh, him," Sue Ellen said. "He's just a brain."

That's bad?

About a half hour later, I suggested again that we circle back. "It gets dark at four-thirty," I told her, "and my aunt gets home at five-thirty, and I have to—"

"There's his car!" she said. "Come on."

I saw the rear of a little gray convertible zip to the top of the hill. "Whose car?"

Right there was when I should have had the guts to turn around. Right when it was dawning on me that I'd been taken. Sue Ellen wasn't out to sell candy. She was out to fake an accidental meeting with Mr. Gessert.

But Sue Ellen is the only girl in this new school who lives near me, so, like a puppy, I followed her up the hill and into an apartment house behind Frontier Village. She'd spotted Mr. Gessert's Fiat in front of the building and rushed inside, checked the mailboxes, and puffed up the stairs. She stopped on the third-floor landing and held on to the rail while her chest heaved in and out under her ski sweater. Sue Ellen's no athlete. The sweater is for looks.

"Why didn't we take the elevator?" I asked her.

"I don't know where it is. And I didn't think you'd want to waste time finding it since you're in such a big rush."

She put the candy boxes down and fumbled in her purse until she found her mirror. "Oh, my hair's a mess. That mousse is a joke. It doesn't stay an hour."

"You look fine," I said. "Let's get going."

"Not everyone has thick, wavy hair like you do, Faith. Here, hold the mirror for me, will you?"

I held the mirror while Sue Ellen pulled strands of her dirty blond hair out from her head until she looked like a frightened chicken. "There," she said, "that's better. We'll start down the hall. You can have the first door."

Nobody answered my knock.

Sue Ellen tried the second door. "Mr. G.! I didn't know you lived here." Her cheeks turned pink as she gazed up into Mr. Gessert's handsome face.

"Well, what are you pretty little girls doing up here?" He looked down at the boxes we were carrying. "Oh-oh, I hate to turn you away, but I already bought two bars at the junior high."

I took a step back. Sue Ellen didn't move. "They freeze perfectly. You can save them for Valentine's Day."

By his fading smile, I could see he didn't know how to get rid of her, so I took another step back. Sue Ellen hung in there.

"Well," he said, "I might have a dollar in my coat pocket."

Sue Ellen moved right up to the doorway. I headed for the stairs.

"Faith!" Mr. Gessert called after me. "Why don't you come in, too. I'll be just a minute."

Once she was in Mr. Gessert's living room, Sue Ellen sat down in a black leather chair. I perched on the footstool, if you could call it a footstool. Like the chair, it had a rosewood frame that curved out into legs. Black canvas was laced to the frame, and a flat cushion lay on top. As I stroked the soft leather, I though how neat the chair would look in my room.

Sue Ellen's beady eyes were taking in every detail. "Wow, check out that stereo," she said, "and those speakers."

The speakers hung from the corners of the ceiling. They looked expensive. Everything in the place looked like it came from the Sharper Image catalog.

Mr. Gessert strolled in from the hall, holding out a dollar bill to Sue Ellen. "OK, I'll try one in the freezer."

After she took the money, opened a candy box, and gave him a chocolate bar, I rose to leave. Sue Ellen rose, too, but instead of walking to the door, she went up to Mr. Gessert. Giving him a simpering grin while carefully keeping her lips closed over her braces, she asked, "May I please use your bathroom before we take that long walk to Lake Stevens?"

He nodded his head toward the hall. "It's down there, to the right."

Sue Ellen trotted off. I sat back down on the footstool. I couldn't think of anything to say, so I just took quick peeks at Mr. Gessert's curly brown hair and broad shoulders while he fiddled with his stereo equipment. Sue Ellen was gone forever. Mr. Gessert dropped the lid down on the turntable. "What's keeping that girl?"

7

I stared at the rug until Mr. Gessert went down the hall after Sue Ellen. "Couldn't you find the bathroom?" His harsh tone brought me to my feet.

"Yes, I did. I was . . . I was . . . I was just looking. . . ."

Mr. Gessert had a red-faced Sue Ellen by the arm when they appeared in the living room. I followed them as he marched her to the door. When he opened it, his cane, which was leaning against the wall, fell to the floor. I bent down to pick it up.

"Leave that alone!" Mr. Gessert dropped Sue Ellen's arm, snatched me by the wrist, and yanked me away from the cane.

"I was . . . I was . . . just trying to pick . . ." I felt as stupid as Sue Ellen as I crowded against her in the doorway.

The anger in Mr. Gessert's face disappeared. "Sorry I yelled at you, but I just finished gluing the handle back on. You understand?"

I nodded, holding my burning wrist, and pushed Sue Ellen into the apartment hallway.

"I only opened the door to one of his rooms," she said in a hurt voice as we walked down the stairs. "I don't understand why he cared."

"What'd you see?" I asked her.

She stopped on the stairway and looked at me, bewildered. "I didn't even get a chance to see anything, and he got so mad. Don't you think that's weird?"

I thought the whole trip was weird.

By the time we got down the hill to the beach, Sue Ellen had Mr. G. transformed into his old adorable self. "Maybe his back rooms are messy, and he doesn't want anyone to know. I don't blame him for not wanting his walking stick broken again, do you?"

I didn't bother to answer her. The sun had gone down, and it was too cold even to talk. I just burrowed on ahead until we got to Twentieth Street, where I said good-bye to Sue Ellen.

The next morning at the lockers, she was the center of attention as she described Mr. Gessert's apartment. Sue Ellen wasn't telling about being kicked out, of course.

Oops, I'll have to finish this letter quick. I just heard the toilet flush downstairs, which means Aunt Linda is up. And if I come down late on Saturday morning when she's already started housecleaning, she won't speak to me. My punishment for being lazy and ungrateful. Guilty. Guilty. Guilty.

Anyway, don't you think Gessert's behavior was strange? I wish I had time to meditate and get some words on him. Oh-oh, I hear water running in the kitchen sink, so I better get up. I can't stand Wheaties and nonfat milk with guilt poured over my head.

Answer this letter right away, please? I'm worried about what is happening to you.

Faith

January 20

Faith,

Keep the envelope this letter came in. My new address is on it. Your last letter was forwarded here. The words you got about me were right on. I have been taken out of the receiving home where I was and put in a foster home.

Everybody threw me a going-away party the night before I left. It was hard leaving all the kids I'd gotten to know, especially since I was with them for four months.

After the party I came to visit you. That must have been the night you felt me in your room. I knew you were hurt and could feel your tweaked-out vibes. When I read your letter, I could see why. I can understand Mr. Gessert getting pissed off at Sue Ellen for poking around in his apartment. The bit about the cane seems a little extreme. Who knows, maybe the guy was just in a bad mood that night, and Sue Ellen set him off.

I've been staying with my new foster parents, Howard and Cynthia Wangsley, for seven days. They live in Seattle, just south of Green Lake. It must be over fifty miles from here to Lake Stevens.

I'm the Wangsleys' first foster kid. They never had any children, either, so it's really quiet here and I'm always alone. Nothing like the old place. I hoped I would be able to make new friends at school.

On the first and second days I went to Jefferson Junior High, I was left to myself. But on the third day, I was coming down the stairs and ran into a big zit-faced kid and his buddies.

"Check this hick out, you guys. Hey, who let you crawl into Jefferson?"

I tried to ignore him and weasel past. He stood on the step below me and blocked my way.

"I'm talking to you." He spat like a drill sergeant, shooting saliva in my face.

Without looking at him, I said quietly, "Please let me by."

He turned toward the fat kid leaning against the stairway railing next to him. "Whoa, he's only been here a few days, and already he's trying to tell me what to do."

The fat kid put his arms around my legs and started to

lift. "C'mon, Rex, let's sizzle him like country bacon."

Rex grabbed my shoulders, keeping me upright, while the rest of his friends helped the fat kid boost me toward the ceiling by my legs.

There was a sprinkler pipe bolted to the ceiling, and as soon as I was close enough to grab it, Rex let go. I started to fall over, so I dropped my books in order to latch onto the pipe with my hands. The sprinkler pipe's brackets ripped out of the ceiling slightly, and I was afraid of tumbling down the steps if the pipe broke loose. Worse yet, I was swinging in plain view of everybody, since a locker area was at the bottom of the stairs.

Suddenly this blond-haired girl stepped out of the crowd. "Leave him alone, you guys. What's he done to any of you?"

They backed away, leaving me dangling from the sprinkler pipe like an idiot.

"Ahhh, how ya doing, Roxanne?" The bully's attitude had changed completely.

"Still picking on people smaller than you, huh, Rex?" She was staring him down even though he was above her on the stairs. "When are you going to get it together?"

"We were just welcoming him to Jefferson."

"Some welcome." She was still looking him in the eye.

"Why you making such a big deal out of it, Roxanne? We didn't hurt him none." Turning around, he slunk after his friends, who had gone up the stairs.

She looked up at me. "Can you drop down?"

I let go and landed with my foot hitting the edge of one

of the steps, almost tipping me down the stairs. I stood up with my face burning.

"Don't feel bad," she told me. "Those assholes pick on anybody who's not somebody. What's your name? Mine's Roxanne."

"Phillip," I whispered.

She was beautiful, Faith. Her hair was blond and smooth as silk clear down to her waist. The deep blue eyes, pink lips, and dark complexion blended perfectly. Her cheekbones and nose reminded me of that statue Roger salvaged in the Gulf of Mexico. When I realized I was standing on the steps open-mouthed, my face got hot again.

Looking away, she said, "Well, I've got to go now. Watch out for those guys."

As Roxanne walked away, I noticed her aura. It was like the bluish purple band of a rainbow had been wrapped around her head and shoulders.

When I got home that evening, I told Cynthia what had happened. She hauled me off to K mart, buying me a polo shirt and new cords, as if that were going to solve the problem.

On the way home, she pulled into a grocery store. "Come on in and help. Let's celebrate with something special tonight."

I got out of the car. "What are you celebrating?"

"Our decision to keep you."

I slammed the door. "I thought you and Howard had already agreed to let me live with you. That's what my caseworker said."

Cynthia came around to my side of the car. "Oh, I'm sorry, Phillip. Howard was supposed to talk to you this morning. He must have been in a hurry to get to the shipyard.

"When we took you, Howard told your caseworker we wanted to wait for a while before making a commitment." She put her hand on my shoulder. "It only took us three days to decide. Come on, let's go shopping."

While I was walking by a cash register, some cans of dog food were moving on the conveyor. I felt like that dog food, stuck on the belt waiting to be checked out. Somebody should have told me I was on a trial basis.

Cynthia let go of the shopping cart she had gotten and said, "Here, you can push it. What's your favorite dinner?"

"Macaroni and cheese," I replied.

"That's a coincidence," she said cheerfully. "We had that the first night you stayed with us. Did you like the cheese omelet I made last night?"

"Yes," I told her, remembering it had been burnt a little.

"I'll make a real dinner tonight." She headed for the meat counter, and I followed with the cart.

"Let's see, we could have chicken, or these spareribs look pretty fresh." She poked at the packages, every so often picking one up and smelling it. "What do you like, Phillip?"

"Anything but meat," I answered.

"You don't like meat? Just wait and see what I can

do. The smell alone will make you hungry."

I wanted to say the smell alone would make me puke, but didn't.

Cynthia grabbed a hunk of red meat. "This looks good. It's been months since we've had chuck roast. Howard will love it." She put it in the shopping cart and moved on down the aisle.

I pushed the cart after her, trying to ignore the meat. She grabbed some potatoes, milk, and a few other items, then took the cart from me and wheeled it up to the checkout stand.

While we were waiting in line, she caught me eyeing a Hershey bar. Taking two of them, she said, "Don't tell Howard. He'll think I'm spoiling you."

On the drive back, neither one of us said much; we just munched on our candy bars.

When we got to the house, Howard's pickup truck was already there. She parked the car, but before getting out, took my candy wrapper out of the grocery bag where I had put it and crumpled it up with hers. Then she covered both of them in tissue paper and dropped the ball in her purse.

I thought to myself: She wanted that chocolate more than I did.

Howard opened the front door just as I was reaching for the doorknob. "How was school today, Phillip?"

"It was OK." I wormed past him and put the bag of groceries on the dining room table.

"Just OK?" He kissed Cynthia on the cheek when she came in behind me. "Where you been, hon?"

She set her bag on the table next to mine. "I took Phillip out and bought him some new pants. Then we stopped by the supermarket on the way back and got a chuck roast for dinner."

Howard walked up behind her. "I thought we agreed on a new budget last night."

She turned around and faced him. "Oh, come on, Howard. We can afford to have a nice dinner tonight, and the kids at school are giving Phillip a hard time about his country clothes. Besides, you never even talked to Phillip this morning like you said you would."

"I know, I'm sorry," he apologized. "I was late this morning, and it slipped my mind."

Through all this, I just stood in the dining room like a stranger. I went and closed the front door, then said to both of them, "I've got homework to do. I'm going up to my room."

I thought neither one of them heard me until Cynthia called after me, "OK, Phillip, I'll call you when dinner is ready."

Going up the stairs, I stubbed my toe on a piece of cracked linoleum that was peeling off the step. It was the same yellow linoleum that covered the sagging kitchen and dining room floors. They sloped so much, if something were spilled in either room, it would run to the low spot and sit between them in a puddle.

You know, Faith, the shabby state of this house and the comment Howard made about budgeting got me thinking. He must make a lot of money at Todd Shipyards, so what's he doing with it?

In my room, I sat down in my chair at the oak desk. This desk is the only cool thing here. It has a cover made out of little strips of wood stapled to cloth. The cover slides in a curved slot over the top of the desk and out of the way when I unlock it. Totally trick.

Howard gave me the key to it yesterday. He told me the other key was lost, and to please hang on to this one. I keep my Edgar Cayce and astral projection books locked in it, hidden away from the Wangsleys. Howard would never bust up his "lovely" desk trying to get in.

I worked on my homework for an hour until it was time to eat. When I opened my bedroom door, the smell of that chuck roast hit me. I swallowed the lump in my throat and went downstairs.

Howard was already sitting at one end of the table after I finished washing my hands. I automatically figured I would sit on the side, because that's where I had sat the last two nights. But when I went to pull up the chair, Howard stopped me. "You sit at the other end."

I tried to ignore how uncomfortable I felt sitting in Cynthia's place. She set the roast on the table, acting like nothing had changed as she sat down herself.

Howard looked across the table at me and asked, "Phillip, would you like to lead us in prayer tonight?"

Here I was staring at a chunk of cooked cow, and he

wanted me to say a prayer. All I could think of was our little calf, Spunky, all chopped up. I focused my eyes on my plate and replied, "I can't."

"Why not?" Howard said, surprised. "Aren't you thankful for the dinner Cynthia prepared tonight?"

I was silent.

"Do you have a problem?" Authority crept into his voice.

Without looking up, I answered, "I'm not thankful for the dead animal on the table."

"What! The Lord put animals on earth for us to eat."

"I believe differently," I said quietly.

"Man has been eating meat for thousands of years," Howard stated. "You think it's wrong to be eating animals? What are we supposed to eat?"

I raised my head. "Fruits and nuts."

"Fruits and nuts!" he repeated. "That's it, nothing else? What about vegetables and grains?"

"Those are okay, too," I said. "But I think humans are designed to live off of fruits and nuts."

"How long have you been on this kick?" Howard asked.

"Since I was in sixth grade."

"No wonder you're so small. Was the rest of your family like this?"

I looked back down at my plate and started to choke up. Cynthia noticed and told Howard quietly, "Dear, I think you should take it easy. His parents died four months ago."

Howard brushed her off. "I want to know. Phillip,

was the rest of your family against meat?"

"No, I'm the only one." That did it. I jumped up and ran upstairs to my room. Cynthia came in and tried to make me feel better.

I could hear Howard down in the dining room. "If that kid wants to eat, he'll learn to eat like the rest of us."

When she asked me what was the matter, I hid my red eyes and mumbled something about Spunky being part of the family. Now she thinks I was upset because I miss the farm and all.

Since that night, Howard always leads the dinner prayer. He and Cynthia belong to some religious group. Last Sunday, the first day I was here, they came home all weirded out. Both of them had been sweating and were kind of wild-eyed.

When Cynthia walked by the only white wall in this house, I got a good look at her aura. It was scattered. In some places it poked way out away from her; in other spots there were holes.

After I saw that, I decided to steer completely clear of their group. I don't want my energy field screwed up like hers. My gut feeling tells me to keep quiet. Besides, they're having a hard enough time trying to accept my vegetarianism.

I'm homesick. Once in a while I wake up in the middle of the night and think I'm on Whidbey Island. Then I realize I'm in another bedroom. Suddenly the whole scene comes crashing in on me. The wreck. Mom, Dad, and Madalyn dead. Aunt Linda rejecting me and the fact that

20

I'm stranded with the Wangsleys. Sometimes I can't stop crying. Why did this happen to us? I just don't get it.

The best part of my life right now is astral projection. I feel so free when I'm out of my body and away from all the hassles. By the way, if you ever want me to stop dropping in unannounced, just let me know. I get kind of lonely sometimes.

Your disconnected twin brother,
Phillip

P.S. I tried to call you, but Howard said it was long distance and cost too much.

January 30

Dear Phillip,

I think of how awful it must be for you to be totally alone, dumped in the middle of strangers. Too bad you can't be with someone like Madalyn's friend Roger. You would have a blast finding sunken treasures on his archaeology trips.

I've tried, but I can't fly around like you do. I can visualize people and sometimes picture what they're doing. I attempted that last night on Mr. Gessert. Sue Ellen had been constantly jabbering about "Mr. G.," which kept reminding me of our trip to his apartment. His behavior in the apartment seemed so out of sync with the too cool teacher that I decided to see if I could figure him out in my head.

After I was settled in bed, I grounded myself by imagining a cord from the bottom of my spine to the center of the earth. Like Roger and Madalyn taught us, I relaxed my body by counting my breaths from one to ten, over and over, seeing each number clearly, until I could no longer feel my hands and arms. It was then I attempted to visualize Mr. Gessert. I felt he was sitting on the floor of his living room with his cane beside him. Only his cane appeared to be in two pieces. This confused me, as he had told Sue Ellen and me that he'd glued the handle on.

My trance slipped away, and I lay in bed trying to make sense of what I had seen. I decided then to go for words and stretched back out, turned up my hands, and began to count my breaths again. When my arms were numb, I asked my question. "Why did Mr. Gessert have his cane apart?"

Clip.

Bullet clip.

Is his cane a gun?!!

Maybe that's why he didn't want me to touch it. But, Phillip, why would a teacher need a gun? Maybe he has a clip that holds the handle to the cane. But why a *bullet* clip?

I wish you were here. I wish so much that we were together, so we could talk things over. It's too bad for us that we don't have any other relatives.

I get angry inside that Aunt Linda didn't think she "could

handle a boy." I try to see it from her old-maid point of view, but it still makes it hard for me to like her sometimes. She sure hasn't liked *me* this week.

Remember I wrote you that my feet were cold? I never ask Aunt Linda for anything because I feel like a charity case since our property on Whidbey Island hasn't been sold yet. She never offers me any money, either.

Well, the old lady next door, Mrs. Tibbets, stopped me coming home from school and asked me if I'd take care of her poodles while she was away for a week visiting her son. I said, "Sure."

I let them out of the basement for a run in the morning, after school, and evening, and cleaned their pen and filled the water bowl. I felt guilty each time I poured kibbles into their dog dishes. Those poodles are so fat they can barely waddle across the street to do their jobs in the neighbors' bushes.

When Mrs. Tibbets got back, she gave me seven dollars. That same day, Saturday, Sue Ellen invited me to ride to Everett with her and her mom. Her mom was taking a couple of old chairs to the thrift shop. After Sue Ellen and I hauled the chairs into the store, we wandered around looking over the junk. There was a bin of shoes and boots marked "five dollars." I found a pair of boots in size six and headed up to the counter, followed by a disgusted Sue Ellen.

All the way home she kept asking me why I wasted my money on secondhand boots that weren't even leather. Sue Ellen's mother, Mrs. Jennings, was shook up by the icy roads and told her daughter to shut up.

I wish I could have told Aunt Linda to shut up. She spotted the package as soon as I came in the door, and I had to show her what was in it.

"What do you want those old things for?" She was sitting in her bentwood rocker drinking a can of Diet Pepsi and reading her copy of *People* magazine. She put her Pepsi on the end table beside the chair and peered over her glasses at my boots. "They've got spots on them."

"I know. I thought I could clean them up."

"It would take a whole can of Energine, which costs more than those boots."

I shifted from one foot to the other. "Well, maybe I could use soap," I said in a little voice.

"Why do you want those clumsy things anyway? Why don't you wear your own boots in this weather instead of going around in tennis shoes?"

"My own boots are too small."

"Oh, come on, now." She flapped her magazine impatiently. "Didn't your mother get you shoes for school this year?"

"We always bought our new shoes at the fall sales instead of in August. But . . . but this year . . ." There was no way I could choke out that this year Mother was dead.

She took a sip of her Pepsi. I would have liked a sip, too, but she had explained to me when I first came that young girls didn't need diet pop. I stood there with a dry mouth, watching her drink.

26

Aunt Linda put the pop down, carefully not looking at me. "Did Mrs. Jennings see you buy those boots?"

"I don't think so. She was busy exchanging the chairs for a night-light."

"She must have seen them when you got in the car. What did you tell her?"

"I didn't tell her anything. She was worried about the slippery roads."

"Listen here, Faith." She looked up at me then. "I don't want you giving the neighbors the impression that I treat you like Cinderella. It isn't necessary to embarrass me. You should have told me you'd outgrown your shoes."

I stood in front of her silently, wondering how I could have brought that up, and wanting to get away from her so bad.

"Well." She lifted her magazine up from her lap. "I'm playing Bingo at the church tonight and eating dinner out with Edith first, so get whatever you want out of the freezer."

I fled for my bedroom.

After Aunt Linda's friend Edith came by for her and I had eaten a chicken pie, I went to work on the boots. I didn't touch the can of Energine. I only used the cleaning stuff at the kitchen sink. First, I sprayed the spots with 409 and then scrubbed the tops of the boots with liquid Ivory soap. I think the sides are made out of padded nylon, and when I rinsed off the soap, the blue fabric shone like new. I didn't dare put the boots by a radiator because the thick soles are made of rubber, but I left them in the

27

bathroom on some newspaper where it would be warm in the night.

From the brightness of the light in my bedroom this morning, I knew it had snowed. And my boots were dry. As I clumped out of the house in them, Aunt Linda didn't say a word. Neither did Sue Ellen as we walked to the junior high, but the kids at the lockers did.

"Moon boots!" Pat exclaimed. "What a neat idea. I wish I had some."

When I got to the social studies class after lunch, Jake was coming in behind me. "Wild boots," he said as he passed me on the way to his seat.

In history, we're up to the western movement. There's a chalk drawing of a big prairie schooner on the front blackboard that Pat did, and the westbound trails on butcher paper on the side bulletin board that Jake did. Mr. Gessert suggested that Jake draw the Hastings Cutoff and the Donner Pass in red, and this day we were to find out why.

When the bell rang and we were seated, Mr. Gessert swaggered in and carefully placed his silver-topped cane in his clothes closet by the door. After Judy had taken roll, he sat on the front edge of his desk, crossed his long legs, and began the story of the Donner party.

"You remember," he said, "that it's two thousand miles from Independence, Missouri, to the Pacific Coast. At fifteen miles a day, which was as fast as the mules or oxen could pull the wagons, the trip took about four and a half months. The emigrants couldn't leave Missouri too early in the spring, because . . . ?"

Pat's hand shot up.

Mr. Gessert nodded.

"Because the grass had to be green for the animals to eat on the way."

"Right!" Mr. Gessert beamed at Pat. Most men teachers beam at Pat. She has almond-shaped eyes and black hair that is cut short except for one long strand that dangles down the back of her neck.

"And if the emigrants stuffed their wagons with too many belongings so the oxen wore out, or the people quarreled along the way, or they took a wrong turn and wasted time, what might happen?" Mr. Gessert called on me, even though I hadn't raised my hand.

"The fall snows might block the mountain passes, especially if they were going over the Sierra Nevada Mountains," I said.

"Rrr-ight!" Mr. Gessert smiled and all the kids smiled back at him, except me, and except Jake, I noticed. "And that's just what happened to the Donner party. In fact, little Virginia Reed, one of the few survivors in the Donner party, wrote a letter after she got to California, advising her cousin not to take any cutoffs and to hurry along as fast as possible."

Mr. Gessert went over to Jake's map then, and pointed out the site of each crisis the Donner party experienced along their way. My mind strayed from Mr. Gessert's lecture at the Hastings shortcut, where for three weeks the emigrants chopped, and shoveled, and pulled, and pushed their way through the Wasatch Mountains.

I was looking at Jake, who was sitting back in his seat with his open-necked shirt showing a few inches of his white chest. I was wondering if his arms were skinny or muscled, when my attention snapped back to Mr. Gessert. The Donner party was now mired in the snow on the top of the Sierra Nevada Mountains. Most of their animals were dead, and all of their food was gone except a tiny bit of flour, sugar, and coffee.

What had caught my attention was the slow, savoring way Mr. Gessert was describing a mother killing the family dog, cooking it, and feeding her children their pet. Pat, who sits in front of me, cringed her head into her shoulders and said, "Oh, ick, I could never. . . ."

Mr. Gessert laughed and said that was only the beginning of the Donner party's strange diet. When they'd eaten all their dead animals and chewed on the hides, and when there were no more mice or twigs or shoes to boil, the survivors began eating their own dead. And, with glittering eyes, Mr. Gessert described how a group of the strongest men and women left the weaker ones in huts and tents and tried to make it out of the Sierras to get help.

It was the middle of December, and before they could make it over the pass they were hit by snowstorms. Their food ran out, and, starving, they talked about killing one of their party so the rest could finish the trip. They decided, instead, to wait until someone died.

When someone did, they ate the dead man's arms and

legs. More snowstorms and more starving, and when Mrs. Fosdick's husband collapsed, another woman cut his liver and heart out of his body, and the sobbing widow had to see her husband's heart roasted over a bonfire.

"Too gross!" came Ray's voice from the other side of the room.

A half smile was on Mr. Gessert's face as he ignored the interruption. He went on to tell what the series of rescue teams from the Sacramento Valley found when they reached the emigrants left in huts and tents up in the mountains.

"What they found," he said, "was a huge hole made by melted snow. At the bottom of the hole was a fire with chunks of a dead woman boiling in a pot. Her little baby daughter cried beside her mother's half-eaten body while the live children and adults lay about in a mess of dirty blankets. There were no dead children above on the snow. The people had eaten them first."

We all stared at Mr. Gessert in an awful silence as he told us of the final rescue team that climbed the Sierras from Sacramento to bring down the last survivor of the Donner party. "His name was Kiesburg, and he was the one, they say, who hung a dead baby from the ceiling of the cabin like a smoked ham." Mr. Gessert still had that half smile on his face, and I shivered and slunk deeper in my seat.

"The rescue party found Kiesburg in a hut with human bones scattered on the floor around three pots. Two pots were full of blood, and another pot held Mrs. Donner's liver. By this time it was nearly spring and the melting snow outside had uncovered a dead ox. When the rescuers asked Kiesburg why he hadn't eaten the ox instead of the woman, Kiesburg said human flesh was more tender."

That was when the classroom door opened and the principal, Mr. Hartman, walked in and took a seat in the back. Mr. Gessert nodded politely and, without missing a beat, concluded his lecture by telling us: "Eighty-seven emigrants from Illinois and surrounding states started out in the Donner party; forty-four of them were children under eighteen. Only forty-seven completed the journey alive."

When the bell rang, ending the period, Jake walked out beside me. "Gessert's crazy," he muttered.

I really think he is, Phillip. It wasn't the gory details of the Donner story. I know they're true. It was the way Mr. Gessert enjoyed telling them that frightened me.

And it must have looked fine to the principal when he came into the classroom to visit. All of the students were paying attention while Mr. Gessert was at the map describing the adventures of the emigrants as they traveled the overland trails to the west.

I wish our family were together again, safe on Whidbey Island. Everything is so scary and wobbly now.

I miss you, twin brother,
Faith

February 7

Faith,

When I read your letter, I got chills all over my body. I went to bed last night thinking about Mr. Gessert, and my thoughts returned to him this morning. When I first woke up, I looked at the alarm clock and it was only 5:30.

Closing my eyes and relaxing, I waited until I got to that point where I sometimes jerk. You know, where the astral body starts to leave the physical body and then snaps back into the physical, making an arm or leg jump. When I felt I could separate, I rolled out of my physical body and sat up in the astral.

I went through my window and headed toward the freeway, staying at streetlight level. On the freeway, I flew north from Seattle until I came to the city of Everett. Solid cars jammed the whole thirty miles or so of freeway I passed over. At Everett, I cut to the east, using the Highway 2 viaduct as a guide.

I circled over Lake Stevens and had just spotted the street Aunt Linda's house is on when I saw a gray sports car barreling up a hill. I followed it to an apartment building and watched this guy get out of the car. When I saw the cane with the silver handle, I figured he must be Mr. Gessert.

Slamming the car door on his coat, he swore and reopened the door. Taking something out of this coat pocket, he inspected it and then put it back. I floated closer to try and get a look in his pocket. His vibes were so creepy, I backed off a bit and kind of hung over his shoulder.

Before I could find out what Mr. Gessert had, I was jolted back to my body by the alarm clock going off. Shaking a bit, I sat up in bed to check the time. An hour had already gone by. Next time I've got to remember to turn the alarm off.

Whatever was in his pocket must have been pretty heavy. It pulled his coat cockeyed across his shoulders.

Yesterday I found out why Jefferson is such a melting pot. Jefferson is an open school. This means kids from all over the Seattle area can come here. Most of the kids from different races and areas of the city get along pretty well together, excluding me.

34

I was coming out of the library with a stack of books a couple days ago when, just my luck, the fat bozo who helped hang me from the pipes discovered me.

"Look what I found, a bookworm. I wonder which book it wiggled out of. This one?" He picked a book from the stack I had and opened it. "Nope, no holes." He threw it on the floor and grabbed another. "Hmmm, don't see any holes in this one." Dropping it, he snatched the next book and opened it with his fat paws. "This book doesn't have any worm holes either. I know bookworms live in books, so where is it?"

Fatso grabbed my shirt and shoved me back against the wall. Now I saw Rex, who had been standing behind us the whole time. "You're not gonna find any books with worm holes in 'em."

Fatso looked at him. "Why's that?"

Rex swaggered up. "Because this is no bookworm you have here. Bookworms have four eyes and wear saddle shoes. Check out the flannel shirt, baggy pants, and waffle stompers. This here's a country worm."

"You know," Fatso said, "I think you're right. It must be a . . ."

"What's going on here!" Mrs. Lillian, the librarian, saved my ass. "Which one of you boys knocked Phillip's books on the floor?"

Fatso let go of my shirt and backed away. Neither one said a word. Mrs. Lillian bored right down on them. "Both of you! Come into the library."

I'm glad she helped me out, but since then I've heard

"country worm" mentioned while walking through the locker area. My new title appears to be catching on.

I definitely stick out here like a railroad tramp in a Nordstrom's department store. This school is smack in the middle of Seattle, and these kids are hard to relate to. They dress differently, act differently, and have a language all their own.

Yesterday I overheard a boy in the halls telling his friend, "I just done a fresh ol' scratch on the back of the gym."

I was afraid to ask anybody what he meant. They'd think I was out of it. Instead I went and looked on the gym wall. There was a scribbled design done with red spray paint. Actually "scribbled" is the wrong word because it was artistic. I'd like to know the kid who made that scratch.

There's another boy in my English class I wish I could be good friends with. His name's Anthony, and he's writing a fantasy fiction book. Even though he pretty much sticks to himself, it amazes me the teacher knows nothing about it. Especially since he's been working on his book since fourth grade!

Our English class is too big for the teacher to control. One day this stubby-haired kid throws a spit wad, and it lands right on Anthony's book. When Anthony flips the guy off, he jumps up and knocks Anthony out of his desk. They must have been fighting on the floor for at least a minute before the teacher broke it up.

The next day, the same obnoxious kid's walking by

Anthony's desk and threatens under his breath, "I'm gonna slime on your book."

Anthony replies out loud, "Just get out of here."

Our teacher turns to him and says, "Anthony, that's why you always get in fights, because you're so, you're so touchy."

You believe that, Faith? The stubby-haired kid's the one causing problems, not Anthony.

Talk about getting picked on, I walked into the lunchroom today and stood looking for a safe place to sit. Suddenly *plop*, somebody hits me in the back of the neck with chocolate pudding. Turning around, I find Rex and his gang laughing.

I got a wet rag from one of the cooks and cleaned myself off. Then I found an empty table in the corner of the room, as far away from Rex as possible. I put my book and lunch sack on the table and sat down with my back to the wall.

I was just reaching in the paper bag for the sandwich Cynthia made, when a piece of cornbread dipped in chocolate pudding skidded off my book and splattered into my face, with the remains falling in my lap.

Before I could get my face cleaned up, a carton of milk sailed past my head and burst against the wall behind me, showering milk everywhere. It made so much noise that Mrs. Budding, the vice principal, jumped. She could see the mark on the wall, but, like me, had no idea who threw the milk.

I got up and faced the corner of the room, away from all the laughing kids. I was almost done wiping my face with a napkin when a voice behind me said. "Do you mind if I eat here?"

I turned around and found Roxanne standing in the puddle of milk. When I just stood there, she went ahead and set her hot-lunch tray on the table next to my book. I watched her sit right down on a glob of chocolate pudding, but was too upset to say anything. She must of missed it while avoiding the milk that was everywhere.

Roxanne picked up my book and started cleaning off the pudding. *"Sixth Sense,* what's this about?"

I finished wiping my chair off and sat down without looking at her. "ESP."

"Is it any good?" she asked.

"I just started it." I turned toward her. "You know if you sit here, you're gonna get hit by food."

"Who's afraid of hot-lunch garbage? Nobody will throw anything if I sit here, anyway. I came over here because I thought we could be friends. You're different from everybody else."

I interrupted her, "Yeah, I'm the kid everybody picks on."

"That's not what I'm talking about, and you know it." She lifted her fork. "Quit sniveling."

"That's easy for you to say. You're beautiful. You got it made."

"A lot you know. Beauty can be a curse. Can you stop being so negative? Or should I go eat my lunch at another table?" Roxanne put her fork down on the tray.

I kind of stepped back and took a look at what I was doing. I was chasing away the only person who had tried to be my friend. What a nut! "I'm sorry I've been acting like an idiot. Things aren't just bad in school; they're screwed where I live, too. I moved into a new foster home."

"Where did you used to live?" Roxanne took her fork and twisted it into the spaghetti in front of her.

"A farm on Whidbey Island," I replied. "My mother, father, and older sister were killed in a car accident four months ago." I pulled the sandwich out of my lunch sack.

"That does sound pretty rough," she remarked before sticking the ball of spaghetti in her mouth.

I unwrapped the sandwich. "I have a twin sister living in Lake Stevens with my aunt," I said, then took a bite.

"Why aren't you living . . . ?"

I gagged and shot my partially chewed mouthful onto the table.

"What's the matter?" Roxanne cried.

"Meat." I choked, grabbing my napkin and spitting the rest of the baloney into it.

"Is it bad?" she asked.

"It is for me."

"Why? Are you allergic to it?"

I scooped up my mess with the paper sack and answered her, "I love animals."

"Then how did the baloney get on your sandwich?"

"Cynthia, my new foster mother, made it. She and her husband have been trying to make me eat meat."

"Why are they doing that?" she inquired.

"Who knows. Maybe they think I'm too skinny, or maybe because they think the Lord created animals for us to eat. I've been there less than a month, and already I'm sick of their trip." I got up. "I need a drink of water. I'll be right back."

After washing my mouth out, I felt better. When I approached our table, I saw the scene I had just left in a new light. Here was this beautiful blond sitting alone at a lunch table surrounded by a totally gross mess. I sat down smiling. Roxanne noticed, and her face brightened in return.

"Do you want my cornbread?" she asked, pushing her tray at me.

"Thanks." I picked up the piece and took a bite.

"So what kinds of books do you like? You read all the time."

"I pick a subject and read everything I can find. I've been through all kinds of things, from rockets to brain waves. I just finished reading some fantasy fiction. First time I've ever read any." I kept quiet about my out-of-body books. Better play it cool.

Roxanne looked at me with interest, "Fantasy, huh. Have you seen Anthony's book?"

"I watch him writing all the time," I said, "but that's it."

Roxanne kept right on talking about Anthony. "No one I know has read Anthony's book. Jefferson's best-kept secret, especially since he's been working on it for so long."

"Have you ever looked at it?" I started wondering if she liked Anthony.

"I asked him once if I could read some, but he told me it wasn't finished. I got the message. Nobody's allowed to mess with his book."

It surprised me that Roxanne was into reading. "What do you like?"

"I like factual books. Adventure, explorers, the country, animals, and even plants. You're from the country; you should feel lucky. Some of the kids in this school have spent their whole life here. I've grown up in Seattle, but my mother takes me to the country whenever she can afford it and find the time."

After Roxanne said this, I was quiet for a moment. I thought about what it would be like to grow up in the city. "How about your dad?"

Roxanne's face clouded for just a second. "What dad? He left my mother before I was born."

"I'm sorry," I said.

She quickly replied, "Don't be. My mother and I have gotten along just fine without him."

The bell for class rang, and we both stood up. I finished the cornbread and wiped my hands on my pants. When I realized Roxanne had seen me do it, my face turned red.

"No biggy," she said, then twirled around on one foot and walked away.

I watched her leave and saw on the back of her white pants a chocolate-pudding stain.

Cynthia is calling for me to go down for dinner now. I'm upstairs in my room at the oak desk. Before I go, Faith, I should tell you my caseworker, Mrs. Langstrom, came by this afternoon. She wanted to know how things were going.

Cynthia told her I was a vegetarian, making cooking for me difficult. Mrs. Langstrom asked me how I was handling that. I explained to her I just eat more food without meat in it. As she was leaving, she suggested that Cynthia might prepare more meals using cheese or eggs.

Cynthia replied, "That's a good idea," and closed the door. Maybe she took my caseworker's advice and made macaroni and cheese tonight. That cornbread for lunch didn't cut it.

Faith, I've stumbled into a black force. After a dinner of scrambled eggs (Cynthia put ham in Howard's), I came up to my room and read for a while, then decided to take another look at what Mr. Gessert was up to. I lay on the bed, separated from my body, and rolled right out of it onto the floor. It even hurt.

I picked myself up and headed for the bedroom window. Instead of passing through like this morning, I bumped right into it. When I pushed against the glass, it felt solid, as if I were still in my physical body.

Walking across the room, I noticed the bedroom door

was ajar. Feeling confined and still wanting to leave the room, I squeezed through the crack. On my way down the stairs, the air became dense. It was like descending into a dark pool of molasses.

After a couple more steps, I could barely move. Straining against it, forcing myself downward, brought me to the point of smothering. It had gotten dark, with grays and browns all around. My attempt to surround myself in light colors failed. The same denseness swirling around my astral body had penetrated my mind.

Realizing I was in over my head, I tried to retreat. The stuff had gotten so thick, I was trapped. I couldn't get away. I began to suffocate. Freaking out, I screamed and slammed back into my body.

Terrifying doesn't describe it. I've got to calm down. I'm shaking so bad, I can hardly write.

If you've ever heard of anything like this, let me know.

Phillip

February 13

Dear Phillip,

I've never read about anyone getting into the gluey place you described, but I do remember Madalyn and Roger talking to us about keeping our thoughts positive. Only those who had similar vibrations could come to us then. Those with lower vibrations couldn't beam in on us.

Maybe it's the same for that space you got into. That school and the Wangsleys had you so down that your negative thoughts sucked you into the glue. Does that sound right?

One time Madalyn caught me swearing because the

sewing-machine thread kept breaking when I was trying to finish an apron for Home Ec. Madalyn told me to go sit in a tree's aura. I chose a big cedar and leaned against the trunk. When the tree's energy calmed me down, an illustration from the instruction booklet came into my head, and it dawned on me that I had put the bobbin into the sewing machine backwards. All I had to do was turn the bobbin around and the thread wouldn't break anymore.

Maybe a tree could help you. Is there a park around where you live? Could you find a big evergreen or a big maple to sit against?

I guess I do have it better than you—at least with Aunt Linda. Mr. Gessert's another thing. Remember old Mrs. Tibbets next door? She trapped me again on my way home from school and asked me if I'd help her with her raspberry bushes. I said sure, because if there is anything I like to eat, it's raspberries.

"Helping" her turned out to mean she stood around with a mug of tea in her hand while I shoveled out stray shoots and cut down the old canes that should have been cut down last fall. She kept saying she just couldn't get everything done in her garden. I know she's not strong, but she'd be better off if she'd bend down and grub in the dirt a little. She's getting as fat as her dogs.

After I had finished and was dripping with sweat, Mrs. Tibbets paid me five dollars and asked me if I'd work three hours for her every week. I didn't answer right away because I was thinking about the raspberry shoots that were still lying on the ground. I'd stuffed the old canes in her trash can.

She hurried on to say she'd pay me ten dollars each time. I said OK, it was a deal, and did she mind if I took the leftover raspberry plants to Aunt Linda's?

"No, no, dear, you're welcome to them. And when we separate the irises and daisies, you can have clumps of those, too." Mrs. Tibbets took a sharp look at me then. "You must be used to having a garden."

I told her I was, that my mother had had lots of flowers on Whidbey Island. The memory left me feeling not too good, so I took the raspberries and went on over to Aunt Linda's and put them in a pail of water.

When Aunt Linda came home, she seemed in a pretty good mood, but, just in case, I waited until we were almost through dinner before I asked, "Would you mind if I put some raspberry bushes in the backyard? I helped Mrs. Tibbets clean out her rows, and she gave me the extra shoots."

Aunt Linda stared at me a moment. I think she needed some time to focus in on raspberries, which wouldn't usually be on her mind. "Well, I guess not," she said. "Just don't make a mess of the whole yard."

"I won't," I assured her. "I'll put them by the north fence. That way they'll get a full day's sun. And a year from this summer, you can have big bowls of raspberries for your breakfast."

She gave me her small, tight smile, but by then I wasn't

feeling too good again because I remembered all those warm mornings on Whidbey when you and I used to go out and pick berries for our breakfast. You remember, too?

After school the next day, I planted the raspberries. When I finished, I stood back by the porch to take in the effect. Sort of bare-looking. Now, if there were flowers beside the outside row . . . So after school the *next* day, I said good-bye to Sue Ellen at the corner of the Mall and went toward Adams Hardware to buy a package of knee-high sweet peas. Just a dollar out of my five. But then, in front of Adams, there were trays of primroses, fifty-nine cents each, and six pots of honeysuckle starts, one ninety-five each.

I planted the sweet peas in the dirt beside the raspberries and my honeysuckle vine against the fence. The three yellow primrose plants I tucked in a foil-lined bread basket, which I set on the coffee table. I was broke, but I felt great. And even greater when Aunt Linda came home.

She saw the primroses first thing. "Oh, how pretty! I love yellow. And what healthy plants." She touched the thick, crisp leaves. "They almost look like salad greens."

That's what I thought, too.

At the dinner table she said suddenly, "You spent your money on the flowers, didn't you?"

"It was worth it," I told her.

"Hmm." She carefully poked her fork into her tuna-fish casserole. "That's what my sister would have done."

Remembering Mother's plump, round figure bobbling

between stalks of dahlias and lilies, her mouth curling in easy smiles, brought me off my flower high fast. Just Mother's smile spread more light than all of Aunt Linda does.

Aunt Linda's feet are too big. No matter what style shoe she wears, they look like gunboats. And her bottom's too fat and her chest's too small. How's that for negative thinking? Maybe it wasn't easy for her to grow up with Mother radiating beside her.

Listen, Phillip, when Mrs. Tibbets gives me the ten dollars each week, I'm going to send five of it to you. Think about it. If you had a chance to earn the money, you'd send half of it to me, wouldn't you? What I'll need my five for next week is some new underpants. I'm *positive* you will be needing things, too. Right? Twins, huh?

I'm going to do my homework in science now, and I'll finish this letter tomorrow. And I've *got* to figure out a science project. All the kids in my room had theirs planned out before I entered the class. I wish I had one of our chickens from Whidbey, so I could make drawings of it— easy project.

February 14

Some Valentine's Day! Ugh. I've been pacing up and down the living room until I've made tread marks on the rug. I'm scared of that Gessert.

Today I was late leaving the junior high because I was talking to the science teacher, Mrs. Thompson, about what project I could do for science. After I left her room, I was walking along the main hall toward the outside door. Mr. Gessert was a couple yards ahead of me. Jake and some other boy I don't know were standing against the wall talking together, when two girls came racing down the corridor. They careened around Jake and his friend and bumped into Mr. Gessert's arm, making his cane fly into the air. As the cane crashed to the floor, I screamed and dived toward the other wall.

One of the girls slid to a stop to pick up the cane and quickly apologize to Mr. Gessert, explaining that she was late for her bus. After she dashed on, Mr. Gessert turned back to me. "What's the matter with you?"

"Oh, nothing." I was trying to regain my cool and saunter down the hall past him. "I'm . . . I'm . . . the loud noise scared me."

He turned in a circle with his dark, cold eyes steadily on me. "Is that so?" He knew I was lying.

I was edging away from him, and he was seeing to it that he kept up with me, never shifting his eyes from my face. My chest tightened, making it difficult to breathe. He was right beside me when I reached the door and felt his hand close around my arm in a hard grip.

"Hey, Faith." Jake pushed open the door from behind us, crowding so close Gessert and I were forced to go on through the entrance. Outside, Jake started rapping away about did I get a chance to see Mrs. Thompson about my science project yet. (He knew I did because I was talking to her when he left the room.) Mr. Gessert watched us silently for a moment, dropped my arm then, and walked on down the front steps and away toward the parking lot.

Jake watched him go. "When he was a kid, I bet he slung cats around telephone poles."

I shivered.

"What was all that about, anyway?" Jake asked as we started down the steps together.

I couldn't think of a good answer, so I kept silent.

Jake raised one eyebrow. "Well?"

I still couldn't think of what to say.

"I've got as much time as you have," he told me and maneuvered our direction so we were headed down toward Lake Stevens beach.

We sat on a log on the beach, watching the ducks mill around. "What's the name of the black ones with the humped backs?" I asked.

"They're coots, I think. Now, what was this about Gessert's walking stick?"

"I think it might be a gun," I blurted out.

Jake looked me over silently.

Cars slowed as they approached the beach area. The ducks are forever waddling back and forth across the road as if they have the right-of-way. The mallards' green feathers shone brilliantly in the February sun, and I wished I lived in a world with no Gesserts and no deaths.

Jake leaned down, picked up a white stone, and tossed it in his hand. "Just how did you come to the conclusion his stick is a gun?"

And so I told him, Phillip. There's something about Jake that reminds me of you. He doesn't look like you.

He's taller, with black eyes instead of blue. And his eyes are set wide in his face, making him look kind of spacy. But I trust him like I trust you.

He didn't act like seeing Gessert in his apartment was any big thing. In fact, he told me about a book his dad bought called *Mind Race,* which has experiments on remote viewing. Jake thought it would be fun if we could practice together some time.

After Jake and I parted at the Mall, I got scared again. I'm still scared, Phillip. I don't know if it's just being torn away from a twin that makes me shaky. Or if Gessert's really evil. Maybe I should find *myself* a tree.

I hope you had a better Valentine's Day than I did. I wish I'd remembered to make you a card.

Faith

February 22

Faith,

It looks like you're on your own with Gessert. I wish I could help you, but I'm still grounded from my last experience. That feeling of darkness is sticking to me. Sitting underneath the biggest tree I could find at Green Lake cleaned my head out, but that's about it. The problem is I have no idea what took place.

In this book beside me on the desk, called *Practical Astral Projection,* the writer had an entity enclose him in a box on the astral plane. He got out by calling upon guides. Even though that's different than what happened to me, I've been asking for help every night before I go to sleep. Maybe nobody's listening, but I figure it's worth a try.

You could be right about negative thoughts sucking me into the blackness. Before I astral-project again, I've got to understand this totally.

When I walked into Mrs. Springfield's history class this morning, I found two display cases full of gold coins. One even had a gold chain in it. I suspected they had something to do with the Spanish, since we've been studying Spain's conquest of the Americas lately. I took my seat just as the bell rang, and seconds later Mrs. Springfield walked in with an elderly, white-haired man who was wearing glasses.

"Class," Mrs. Springfield said, "today we have a special treat. Dr. Rassmussen is a distinguished underwater archaeologist who has done remarkable work. He has agreed to visit our class and show us some of the artifacts he and his colleagues have raised from Spanish galleons. After his presentation, you may ask him questions. Dr. Rassmussen, they're all yours."

"Thank you, Mrs. Springfield. Well, I don't know how distinguished I am. I view myself as somebody who just likes finding sunken treasure. The older the better. My favorite place to search is the Caribbean."

I leaned forward in my seat, wondering if he knew Roger.

Dr. Rassmussen went on, "Actually, my most rewarding work has taken place off the Silver Shoals of the Dominican Republic."

I remembered hearing Roger talking about the Silver Shoals. I raised my hand and blurted, "Have you ever heard of a man named Roger Clinton? He's an underwater archaeologist, too." Suddenly it was quiet. I had butted in.

Mrs. Springfield looked shocked. "Phillip, I said you may ask questions *after* Dr. Rassmussen is through."

Dr. Rassmussen turned toward her. "It's all right, Mrs. Springfield. Actually, Phillip, I think I have heard of him. Isn't he a little unorthodox? Supposedly using psychic means to find wrecks. I've never met him, but some of my colleagues have. Why do you ask?"

I slouched down in my seat, bummed. "Oh, nothing." I had hoped he knew where Roger was. Dr. Rassmussen looked at me funny for a second, then went on talking.

His big deal was the gold chain which was worn by some Spanish captain. The rest of what he said went past me. My mind was busy trying to figure out how to get ahold of Roger. When I left the class, I heard Mrs. Springfield say the cases were going to be moved up to the library so other kids could see them.

At lunch, I told Roxanne about the displays. She wanted to look at them, so we finished eating and headed upstairs to the library. As we were climbing the steps, she turned to me. "I'm reading *Sixth Sense* now. Do you believe it's possible to learn how to leave your body and fly around?"

I like Roxanne a lot. The thought of her getting stuck in that goo gave me the creeps. I wished she had never seen me reading that book. "Anything's possible, but I only take something like that seriously if I experience it myself."

Roxanne replied, "I think astral projection is real. Remember the story about the girl who left her body and found her friend sick, then called for help?"

"Yeah," I said.

"When I read it, I got goose bumps. I have a feeling the story's true."

Roxanne was looking at me so earnestly, I wanted to tell her all I knew. Instead, as we walked through the library doors, I repeated, "Anything's possible."

We headed toward the rear of the library, where a bunch of kids and two adults were gathered around the displays. One adult was Mrs. Lillian, and the back of the other struck a chord of familiarity. When he spoke, I froze.

"I want to thank you for letting the librarian at Lake Stevens know these coins were going to be here today. Otherwise I wouldn't have known this collection was going to be present in the Puget Sound area."

"Phillip, Phillip, what's the matter?" Roxanne was tugging on my shirt.

"Just listen," I whispered. Taking her hand, I guided her in between the bookshelves where we could watch unnoticed.

"Who's that?" Roxanne asked.

"His name is Mr. Gessert," I said quietly.

Mrs. Lillian began speaking to Gessert. "When I told your librarian about this, she mentioned your interest in the Spanish. I think it was awfully sweet of her to take over the rest of your classes for the day, don't you, Mr. Gessert?"

With no show of feeling, he answered, "Yes, it was."

Mrs. Lillian went on, "This is quite a collection. I believe this is the most valuable thing I've ever had in my library."

Mr. Gessert bent over the cases. "It is amazing, especially the chain. Solid gold, molded into form hundreds of years ago by the hands of Spanish goldsmiths. I wonder how much it weighs?"

"I have no idea," Mrs. Lillian replied.

He straightened up. "Well, I'd best get going. I still have some things to do before going back to Lake Stevens. Thank you again for giving me the opportunity to see these artifacts."

Mrs. Lillian walked with him toward the front of the library.

Roxanne turned me toward her. "What's all that about?"

I was trying to figure out how to explain, when we were distracted.

"I'm telling you, Rex, I saw this thing when they hauled it into the library. Talk about a treasure. It blows me away they brought it here." The fat kid came yapping though the doors behind Rex.

Rex jostled the other kids aside and planted himself in front of a glass case and began checking each piece out. When he finished one case, he started on the second until he came to the chain.

He elbowed the fat kid. "Man, look at that thing. I could throw a kick-ass party with the cash it would bring."

"Where would you get rid of it?" Fatso asked.

"I got my connections, and I ain't telling you." Leaving the cases, he started walking toward the library doors, but stopped when he spotted Roxanne and me watching him. He came over, acting like she was alone. "What's happenin', girl?"

Roxanne ignored him.

"You want to go to the Laserium Saturday night? It's Pink Floyd."

She looked right through him. "Rex, I wouldn't go anywhere with you."

His face turned beet red. "You've made a mistake, lady. This country worm you're screwing with is the nerd. And you better watch it, or he'll rub off on you. Then you'll be worming your way through Jefferson, too." With that, he spun around and left the library, leaving the fat kid standing alone.

Roxanne looked at me. "He seems a bit upset."

"Just a little perturbed," I added.

After my last class, I headed out of the building, thinking about Roxanne. My thoughts were interrupted by sirens approaching the school. They stopped on the east side of the school, so I went around to see what was going on.

By the time I got there, the cops had already roped off the area around a dark blue van. Dr. Rassmussen was inside the barricade talking to a cop. The back door of the van was open, and the window in it was smashed.

When I tried to find out what was going on, a teacher ordered me away from the area. I was walking past the entrance of the school as Roxanne came running down the steps. "I heard the principal telling a teacher the chain and some gold coins have been stolen. Dr. Rassmussen took the display case with the chain in it down to his van first and locked it up. While he was going back for the second case, somebody busted in and took the coins and chain."

"Do they know who did it?" I asked.

"No way. It could have been Rex. You heard what he said."

While Roxanne was telling me this, I was wondering if it was just a coincidence that Mr. Gessert came to our school today.

Cynthia just walked into my room to tell me dinner is ready. I quickly covered the astral projection book up with the pages of this letter. She asked me what I was doing. I looked up and told her I was writing you about the robbery. That seemed to satisfy her because she left. She may have seen the book, though. I'd best lock it up in the desk and go down to eat.

It's Sunday now, Faith. I had an incredible dream early this morning, if it was a dream. Anyway, here's what happened.

There was another door leading out of my bedroom. I

was looking for somebody, and when I opened the door, it led to a hallway that entered into a room.

A man was sitting in the middle of the floor. His thin beard came clear down his chest, and he had long white hair tumbling onto a flowing white robe. I noticed the only light in the place seemed to be radiating from him. He didn't say a word when I walked in, just gazed at me with piercing dark eyes. Without thinking, I said, "I need help."

Standing up, he motioned for me to follow. We walked out of the room and into mine! He led me down the stairs and on into the living room. Still silent, he signaled for me to be seated on the couch.

Sitting on the coffee table, he picked up a magazine and ran his hand across the front cover. Where the tips of his fingers touched, the paper became light. I was utterly amazed.

He made a fist with his hand and held it in front of me. Turning it over, he opened it palm up, and there, in the middle of his hand, was a ball of pure white light.

Looking right into my eyes, he said, "Listen to what goes on around you. Behind every sound you hear will be another which can be heard inside your head. I call it the Current of Sound. Others give it different names, such as the Music of the Spheres or the Word.

"Once you are able to hear the Current, listen to it as you're getting ready to go to sleep. Then gently repeat the word *Hu*, drawing it out slowly like this: *Huu-u-u-u.*"

The whole room reverberated from the vibrations of

his voice. I became light-headed and felt like I was lifting off the couch.

He stopped *Hu*-ing and explained, "Suddenly, you will be aware you're asleep, somewhat similar to realizing you're dreaming in a dream. The Current of Sound and the repetition of *Hu* are like a thread, pulling you past the boundary of sleep into another plane or dimension. This is one way to travel as Soul, which is different from astral projection. When traveling as Soul, the astral body stays behind with the physical body." He finished speaking and stood up.

"It's that simple?" I asked

"Yes."

I was so delighted, I wanted to give him a big hug. Feeling shy, I held out my hand instead. "Thanks a lot."

He stepped forward and embraced me. I wrapped my arms around him in return. Love washed through me, leaving a tingling sensation when he let go.

"Green Lake would be a good place to practice hearing the Current of Sound. I'll be there tomorrow morning." He began to fade right before me, then became distinct again. "One more thing. Think before you speak to anyone about your experiences with traveling as Soul. Why are you telling them? And what good will it do? Use the little feeling inside that tells you what is right and wrong."

I woke up in bed with the feeling of his presence surrounding me. This may sound crazy, but when he was holding that beautiful ball of white light, somehow I knew it was truth. The whole experience was realer than life.

On the way downstairs for breakfast, I told myself I had to get to Green Lake. As I walked into the front room, Cynthia had just completed ironing one of my good shirts. I went into the bathroom to wash my hands. She called after me, "Phillip, wash your face and neck so you will look nice today."

I thought to myself, Oh no, here come the screws. After finishing in the bathroom, I sat down at the breakfast table. Howard walked into the dining room, all decked out. Knowing full well what they were up to, I decided the best approach was to feign ignorance. I looked at Cynthia and asked, "What's the big occasion?"

She hurried to the table with a steaming pan of scrambled eggs and replied, "We're all going to the Group this morning."

Howard sat down at the table. "Afterwards I thought you and I could go over to Jefferson and shoot some baskets."

"How long will you be gone?" I was thinking as fast as I could, trying to figure a way out of this.

Cynthia answered cheerfully, "We'll just be at the Group a couple of hours—then you and Howard can go play."

"I'm sorry, I have to go to Green Lake."

"Why is that?" she asked.

"There's a guy I gotta see," I replied.

"Do I know him?"

"No."

"Well, that's okay, Phillip. He can come, too. I'll give him a call and invite him along." She walked over to the phone and took it off the hook. "What's his name and number?"

"I've only known him a little while. I think it would be wrong to welch out." What can I say, Faith? It was the best I could do on short notice.

Howard had been listening quietly. "Phillip, Cynthia and I would really like you to come to the Group with us today. We feed you, clothe you, and give you a bed to sleep in. The least you can do is try and help us make a family."

"I have to go. I've already said I would meet him at Green Lake." I know it was kind of a lie, but I was getting desperate.

Howard replied, "You knew we wanted you to come to the Group. Just call your friend after breakfast and tell him you will be a little late."

I shut up. After breakfast, I pretended to make a phone call, then came upstairs. Cynthia must have spotted that astral projection book on Friday night, all right. If I can't get out of this, I'll never know if the man with the white light is really going to be at Green Lake.

I'll stay in touch.

Much Love,
Phillip

March 16

Dear Phillip,

I've been waiting and waiting to hear from you. The end of your last letter sure left me hanging. I tried calling you last night, but the man that answered said you were in bed. Now I still don't know if you went to Cynthia and Howard's Group or met the "man" at Green Lake???

You're lucky Gessert didn't show up at Green Lake. Or the ducks are lucky. He has to be the meanest man living. Today he killed a beautiful mallard and crippled two others. He makes me sick.

It happened early this morning when Sue Ellen and I were peddling the remains of our band candy, trying to catch kids at home who'd whine their mothers into buying some. We'd gotten rid of the last box at a big brown house across from Lake Stevens. Coming down the steps, I started to say to Sue Ellen, "Well, we can finally dump these dumb carrying cases," when I saw Gessert's car wheel down the road in front of us.

You're only supposed to go twenty-five miles an hour in Lake Stevens. Everyone goes even slower for the ducks that hang around the swimming beach. Gessert was doing at least fifty and plowed right through a line of ducks that were waddling across the street.

I raced down the rest of the steps and picked up a mallard. Its head hung over my arm while its bill slowly opened and closed. Sue Ellen tried to catch the two who were limping toward the water, but they edged away from her. She came back to where I was stroking the mallard's feathers and stood beside me, objecting to my cursing Gessert. "Maybe he was late for a meeting or something and didn't see the ducks."

"A likely story. He can see as well as any other driver." I started walking fast toward the junor high, thinking maybe Mrs. Thompson could save the duck's life. Its bill was still moving, even if its eyes were closed and its body was limp.

Sue Ellen trotted beside me. "You don't know Mr. G. saw the ducks. Maybe he couldn't brake in time."

"Shut up," I told her and walked even faster. I no longer cared if she was one of the few kids I knew around school. She's an idiot.

Mrs. Thompson wasn't in her room when I got there.

I patted the gleaming green feathers on the mallard's head while I waited. He was so pretty, so soft and pretty. I kept watching his bill, hoping he'd open it again. Maybe he wouldn't die if he kept breathing. I stroked his chestnut breast and rubbed my fingers around the white collar on his neck.

Mrs. Thompson bustled into the room, hung her coat in the closet, and came over to where I was standing by her desk. "What have you got there?" she asked me.

I held the duck out to her. "A mallard Mr. Gessert ran over on the beach road. Do you think it'll live?"

She felt the duck's chest and pried open one of its eyes. "No, honey. I'm afraid it's dead."

"I hate that man. I hate that mean man." I could feel my mouth turning down, my throat tightening. I wiped my sleeve across my eyes.

Mrs. Thompson laid the mallard down on her desk and put her arm around me. "Maybe he didn't see the duck. We had a faculty meeting this morning, and he was late."

"Maybe he wouldn't have seen one, but he hit a whole line of them crossing the street. He's just plain cruel."

For a moment there was a distant, calculating look in Mrs. Thompson's eyes, and then she shook herself and me and asked in a cheerful voice, "Well, what good thing could we do for the duck?"

"I could draw him," I said. "I could draw all the parts of his body—the feathers, and the webbed feet, and his yellow-green bill. And I could look up in the bird books about mallards and label my drawings correctly."

Mrs. Thompson nodded. "That's a fine science project for you. We'll keep him in the classroom refrigerator, except when you're using him for a model. Do you think you could get your drawings finished in a week?"

"Sure," I said, "I'm good at drawing." And then I felt a little embarrassed, but Mrs. Thompson didn't seem to think I was bragging. She just had the nice smile on her plump, sweet face as she put the duck in the refrigerator. Her first-period kids were wandering in by then, so I went off to my English class.

Miss Bowen, the English teacher, started us on a journalism unit. Each of us is to interview someone in the school and write it up for the ninth-grade newspaper. Jake chose the janitor, I chose Mrs. Thompson, and Sue Ellen chose Mr. Gessert, of course.

After school, Sue Ellen came into the science room when I was interviewing Mrs. Thompson. I was sitting on one of the desks in front of the room. Mrs. Thompson had her chair tilted back to the blackboard while she told me how she'd always wanted five children.

"Why five?" I asked her.

"Seemed like a nice fat amount. Lots of children around the Christmas tree. Lots of squealing when they found their Easter baskets at the end of their beds."

"So how many did you have?"

Mrs. Thompson leaned her head to the side, shrugging her shoulders. "None."

"None? Why?"

"Because it turned out that my husband and I couldn't have children."

"Ohh." What a dirty trick, I was thinking to myself. She'd make such a nice mother.

Sue Ellen left the doorway and edged toward Mrs. Thompson's desk. "There are five kids in my family."

"So?" I said. I didn't want Sue Ellen butting in on my interview. She stood there uncertainly, not coming any closer.

When I was sure I had her backed off, I gave my full attention to Mrs. Thompson. "You could have adopted some children."

"I thought of that," she agreed. "But then I saw an ad for a wolf hybrid in the paper, and I'd always wanted a wolf, so I bought the puppy, and then I bought a female to keep him company, and then they had puppies. . . ." She smiled her warm smile at me.

I was so interested in someone having a wolf that I bent forward, almost tipping the desk over. "Are they fierce?"

"No, wolves are intelligent, loving, family-oriented animals. They're friskier and bigger than most full-blooded dogs, but we have twenty acres, so that's no problem."

Boy, wouldn't it be neat to have a wolf, Phillip? I was wishing I had Mrs. Thompson for a foster mother when Sue Ellen put in, "We have a Persian cat."

I didn't dare say "Who cares?" to shut her up again, and Mrs. Thompson thumped her chair down and started straightening the papers on the top of her desk, so I knew it was the end of the interview. On the way out of the science room, Sue Ellen asked me if I'd go to Mr. Gessert's classroom with her. "Not a chance," I told her.

"Well, I came in while you interviewed Mrs. Thompson," she said.

"All that did," I told her, "was keep me from finding out more about wolf hybrids, which would have made a real good story."

"Oh, you can ask her some more questions tomorrow. And, anyway, everyone will want to know about Mr. G."

"Good luck," I told her and walked on out the school doors.

When I was about halfway home, Sue Ellen came puffing up. "Was he fascinating?" I asked her.

"He was ready to go home, so he couldn't talk long. I shouldn't have waited for you," she added resentfully.

"Too bad," I said. "Did he want to have five kids, too?"

"No, he said he doesn't believe in marriage. I asked him if he taught school so the kids could be his children, and he laughed and said he taught school because the only college scholarship he could get was in education."

Figures, I thought to myself. I didn't say it to Sue Ellen, though. She's a complete airhead, but it will get through even to her that I don't like her if I keep being mean, and I don't need another enemy. Gessert's enough.

I wish I had a loving wolf to put my arms around right

now. Aunt Linda's lived alone so long, she has all the feelings of a big stuffed doll.

I miss you,
Faith

PS. I'm enclosing ten dollars for your half of the money I've gotten from Mrs. Tibbets the last two weeks.

March 20

Faith,

I read your letter and was horrified. Killing one duck is bad enough, but smashing into a whole line of them and leaving some injured, that's absolutely gross. His Karma will catch up with him, just watch.

You know what I did the Sunday Howard was trying to take me to the Group? I went inside the bathroom, then slipped out the window and went down to Green Lake.

When I got there, my adrenaline was pumping. I found a fir tree and leaned against it with my eyes closed. Quite a few kids were playing on the dock. All of their shouting and laughter blended together. I tried to listen behind the constant noise they made, but kept wondering if the man in my dream was real. If he was real, would he show up?

After a bit, my mind wandered to the waves lapping the shore of the lake. They sounded kind of cool and relaxed me. Once I thought I heard something inside my head. But then I listened really hard and it disappeared.

When I gave up and opened my eyes, in the mud, right in front of my feet, were footprints. Whoever they belonged to had made less noise than the wind.

Following the tracks with my eyes, I could see they led to a middle-aged man dressed in gray slacks and a blue sweatshirt. I was just thinking, he looks like the typical family man, when suddenly he started stripping off his pants. I thought he must be a flasher until I saw his swimming trunks and realized he was actually going swimming in February.

After he had been in the water about twenty minutes, he got out, dressed, and started walking back the way he had come. When he was right in front of me, he stopped and said hello.

It bothered me having a complete stranger standing over me as I was sitting down against the tree. I peered up at him uneasily and stayed silent.

A couple of seconds went by, and then he asked, "Do you recognize me?"

"No," I answered.

He held his right hand out front, clenched into a fist, then turned it over and opened it palm up. Talk about blown away. I looked at his face closely and saw he had the same dark, piercing eyes as the guy with the ball of light. I blurted, "You're the man from my dream last night."

He looked at me, smiling. "What dream?"

"What happened to the long hair and robe?"

"That was what you expected a teacher to look like. May I sit down?"

"Sure," I said. He was carrying a blue nylon day pack. Dropping it on the ground, he seated himself next to it. His appearance was so ordinary, it bothered me. He even had on sneakers. Somehow I expected a wise man, teacher, or whatever he was, to be more majestic. The only thing special about him were his eyes. "How did you get into my dream?"

"Whoa, hold it. You're the one who asked for help. I'll enter somebody's space only if I'm invited. You were traveling as Soul when you approached me."

"I was?"

His face broke into a grin, and little crinkles appeared around his sparkling eyes. "Yeah, most people do. Thing is, they're unaware of it. The trick is to become conscious of traveling as Soul, and then learn how to control it."

"How long does it take to do that?" I was thinking he must really be a master at it in order to travel from wherever I met him to Wangsleys' living room.

"It depends on the person. Besides, I'm still getting better and probably always will. I can give you a little tip. Remember when I asked you to follow me?"

"Uh-huh."

"You kept your attention on me, right? When I went down the stairs into the living room, you came along. Anywhere else I would have gone, you would have gone, too, simply because you were focused on me. Wherever you anchor your attention, whether it be a person, place, or thing, you'll be. Anchor points can be used to hold yourself steady, as well as to move around."

He started to unzip his day pack. I watched him curiously, wondering what sorts of things he kept in it. He pulled a brown paper bag out and handed it to me. "Here, I brought you a present." After I took it from him, he stood up. "Time to go."

I lifted my eyes toward him and said, "What is it?"

"Open it up, and you'll find out."

I reached into the bag and took out a paperback book. It was called *In My Soul I Am Free,* and I recognized the name of the author. "I've heard of Brad Steiger."

When there was no reply, I raised my head and discovered he was gone. Jumping up, I looked around and then went behind the tree. He was nowhere to be found. I wish I could have at least got his name.

Well, Faith, I bet you want to know what happened to me when I went back to the Wangsleys' and faced the music for slipping out the bathroom window. Howard was pissed. First he sat me down and gave me a big lecture about honesty. Then he made me stand in the living room for half an hour trying to hold up two books with my arms outstretched.

After fifteen minutes, my muscles gave out. Every time

my arms started slowly sagging toward the floor, Howard would grab ahold of the books, shove them up in the air, and say, "I said hold them up!" As far as I'm concerned, Howard's a fanatic hanging way out in the wings.

Even though I got in trouble for sneaking down to Green Lake, it was worth it. I'm still trying to get the hang of traveling as Soul, although now I can hear the Current of Sound.

The first time, I was lying in bed and it was windy outside. I listened to the wind for a while and, at the same time, tried to hear it in my head. There was nothing like the wind, but slowly I began to notice a sound a little bit similar, with a higher pitch.

As I kept listening, a much clearer sound came to me. It was just like the sea heard inside a conch shell. The longer I listened to it, the better I felt inside. Kind of a clean, warm feeling like nothing I've ever experienced before. Now the sound comes whenever I'm listening for it, and even sometimes when I'm not.

The Current of Sound got really loud while I was reading some more of *Practical Astral Projection*. The author was describing what it was like going down into the lower astral plane.

The farther he went, the thicker and denser it got. Pretty soon he was having trouble moving and was afraid of getting stuck.

I'm not quite sure why the Current of Sound came on so strong. Maybe it was trying to tell me I had stumbled into the lower astral plane.

This may sound a bit weird, Faith, but I feel like when the Sound gets really loud, I should pay attention to what's going on. And today, when the Current of Sound appeared inside my head again, that's what I did.

Roxanne and I were cutting through Washington High School, or what used to be Washington High. It's abandoned now. We were passing through the central courtyard when the Sound started ringing in my ears. At that moment, Roxanne turned to me. "Does this place ever give you the creeps?"

"Yeah, it does. Sometimes it's like a ghost town, so quiet and spooky." I got an impression of the towering red brick walls behind Roxanne tumbling down and trapping her in their clutches.

Roxanne began moving faster and said, "These broken windows and ivy-covered walls remind me of a horror movie. It's freaking me out. Let's get out of here."

By the time we'd cleared Washington's grounds, the Current of Sound had disappeared. I made a mental note to stay away from that place. I slowed down and asked her, "Have you heard anything about the robbery?"

She matched my pace. "While I was working in the office, I overheard the principal telling my P.E. teacher no fingerprints were found on the truck or display cases. The police still think one of the kids stole the chain and coins."

Roxanne looked down and shifted her books from one arm to the other. When she lifted her head back up, the sunlight shone on her face. I was struck by her beauty.

And on top of her killer looks, I knew she had a golden heart. I really like her.

She asked me, "Did you know Rex is throwing a free party at a friend's house Friday night?"

"No, I'm not too well connected to the grapevine. I wonder where he got the money."

The wind was blowing Roxanne's hair around her neck. "Maybe he took the gold," she said. "He doesn't strike me as that daring, but who knows."

We had come to Roxanne's house. She took my hand and squeezed it. "Thanks a lot for walking me home. Do you want to come in for a minute?"

"I'd better get going. The Wangsleys will be tweaking out if I'm late. See you at school tomorrow."

I wish I'd had the nerve to go in. Too shy, I guess. Oh well, I'm getting over it slowly.

Thanks a lot for the ten dollars. I'll use some of it to call you this Saturday as close to three o'clock as possible. I'm not sure how long it will take me to walk to a pay phone.

Time for bed. It's after twelve o'clock.

Miss you,
Phillip

PS. It's happened this morning! I've traveled as Soul.

79

April 5

Dear Phillip,

Hey, that was neat talking to you on the phone. Not as good as seeing you, but it sure beats letters. After we hung up, I remembered that sometimes at night when I'm in bed, I hear a ringing. Mostly it comes in my left ear. It doesn't sound like the ocean, but it does sound like a current. And then sometimes there's a faint noise all around me like the atmosphere. I felt like calling you right back to tell you about it, but how could I call back to a pay phone? Stuck!

The teacher-man's advice about keeping your mouth shut seems right on. I doubt if straight old Cynthia or

Howard could handle it. And I don't think Howard's as righteous as he would like you to believe, either. Remember what he said about feeding and clothing you? They do, of course, but he made it sound like a bigger deal than I think it is. I think they get paid for taking care of you.

I noticed Aunt Linda gets letters from the same insurance company Mom had. She got one of them today, and I said, "Do you have the same insurance company as my folks?"

She looked at me, sort of irritated, and said, "No."

"Well, isn't that a bill from the same company?"

"It isn't a bill," she said. "It's a check."

"How come it's a check? I thought . . ."

"It's a check from your parents' insurance company to provide for you."

"Oh." I had thought there wouldn't be any money for us until the farm was sold. I thought we were sort of paupers. "I didn't know I had any money."

"It's to take care of you." She sounded even more irritated. "You're not getting cheated."

I backed away from her. "I didn't mean I was getting cheated. I just thought you were giving. . . ." I started for the kitchen to set the table for dinner. It was safer.

When we sat down to eat, she asked me, "Why are you still clunking around in those boots? It isn't going to snow in April."

I looked down at the scruffy boots. "In a couple of weeks, I'll have saved enough of Mrs. Tibbets's money to get a pair of tennis shoes." This was true, but I said it on purpose, because if there was money to care for me, didn't it include clothes?

My innocent, eager little voice didn't fool old Linda. "Oh, for heaven's sake. I'll take you shopping tomorrow, since it's Saturday."

I'm half glad she's taking me shopping and half pissed she hasn't done it before. She can't be that forgetful of my growing body. I live in the same house with her.

I'll finish this tomorrow. I'm going to spend some time labeling my science drawings before I go to bed. I brought the duck pictures home and a book about water birds.

Saturday night

Two good things happened today. One for you and one for me.

The one for you is that we got a letter from *Florida!* from Roger! He thought we were living together and sent the letter here in care of Aunt Linda. I guess when he left after the funeral, he must have assumed she would take us both. He said he was sorry he couldn't have stayed with us longer and talked to us a little more.

If he only had, he would have known you were going to be put into a foster home. Anyway, you can write to him now. I'm enclosing his letter.

The good thing that happened to me was that Aunt Linda did buy me some neat clothes. She really got into it. After she picked out three bikini underpants (with hearts on them!), she bought me jeans and two blouses, and then saw a fire-engine-red cotton sweater that she thought would look neat with my brown eyes. And it did, too. Especially in my new bra that doesn't smash my chest flat like the ones I've grown out of.

When we'd finished shopping, Aunt Linda took me to Skippers for fish and chips. She felt so good about finding me red moccasins to go with the sweater that she couldn't stop chattering. I thought she looked almost pretty with her eyes all shiny while she was telling how she had spied the red shoes and pounced on them.

After she'd run on awhile, she turned sort of pensive. She had a French fry in her fingers and dangled it into a paper cup of ketchup. "You know, Faith, I was a bit jealous of my sis . . . your mother. It always seemed to me that she got everything. I would have liked to have a little girl to dress and take places. . . ." Aunt Linda ate the French fry slowly, looking vacantly over the booth, and then shook herself. "Anyway, everything changes."

I guess it does, huh, Phillip?

Good night, twin brother.

Monday

Do Cynthia and Howard get the *Seattle Times?* In case they don't or in case you didn't see it, I'm enclosing a news story about a black-masked robber. Get the part that says "a man was seen driving away in a gray sports car shortly after the time of the robbery." A coin shop was robbed. Get that, a coin shop. It had to be Gessert.

I hope they catch him. I hope he gets shot. No, no. Erase that. I don't really hope that. Well, maybe I do, but I know I'm not supposed to say so.

I went to school this morning all clipperty-lip. I was dressed up in my red sweater and red shoes and new jeans. The girls at the lockers said, "Whoa, don't you look great!"

I waved my head around and told them my Aunt Linda finally broke loose with some clothes that fit. Guilt tugged at me, flashing on how Linda got off on getting me the stuff, but that's how you act in junior high, so that's how I acted.

Sue Ellen stood at the edge of the group with her green glass earrings dangling through her prickly hair. Remembering her jealous eyes now makes me admit sometimes I don't act any better than she does. But I'm not always that bad. I think when Mom and Dad and Madalyn died, we lost our rudder. I'm amazed that you snuck out a window.

At lunch I was still feeling grand, so I upped myself out of the girls' ninth-grade table and walked over to Jake at the boys' table. I leaned over Jake's shoulder and put the news clipping in front of his nose. "I bet I know who this is," I said. "We could check it out after school."

"Uh, OK," he said. I knew he didn't get it, but he would later.

Still feeling good, I went into Gessert's class and put my social studies book on the center of my desk and my science project on the upper corner. This was the day we silently read a chapter before having a class discussion. Gessert says we do it this way so everyone will be prepared. I think we do it this way so he'll have time to read the chapter, too.

Only he was restless and, instead of reading his book, he wandered around the room. When he came to my desk, he started poking through my science drawings. He's nosy like that. "What are these pictures for anyway?" he asked. "Ducks?"

"It's my science project." Apprehension made my voice squeak.

"Mandible? Mandible?" He made the word sound like it was dirty. "What is this *mandible?* What's wrong with duck's bill?"

"It's the lower part of the duck's bill," I murmured, my face burning hot.

"Ohhh, the *lower* part of a duck's bill. Isn't that interesting. And she gives you credit for drawing these little Disney characters?" He turned away from me and strode on down the aisle. I sat there for the rest of the reading time, totally humiliated, not daring to look at anyone.

Sue Ellen met me at the lockers after school. "I don't think Mr. G. likes you," she said.

"You noticed. Good for you." I brushed past her and hurried toward the outside doors. I hoped I wasn't going too fast for Jake to catch up with me. I wasn't. He was waiting on the school steps.

"Oh, I hate him, I hate him," I said through my teeth.

Jake grinned. "I think it's mutual."

"So Sue Ellen told me." I stopped on the bottom step and looked up at him. "How much time have you got?"

"How ever much it takes."

"Good." As we walked along, I was thinking. Where was a place that people wouldn't stare at us? There was no privacy along the lake. Easy! "Let's go sit in my backyard."

Jake threw up his hands, meaning *I don't get it, but OK.*

I opened the front door of Aunt Linda's house with my key and dumped my books on the dining room table. Jake followed me through the kitchen and out the back door to the yard. "I don't know how good cherry trees are for this, but it will have to do," I said. "You sit on that side, and I'll sit on this side. Lean against the tree and try to relax." I wiggled close to the trunk, closed my eyes, and took three deep breaths.

"Ahhh, I don't want to disturb the ambiance here," Jake whispered, "but what are we doing?"

My eyes flew open. "Oh, I thought we'd relax first. But maybe it's a good idea if you start thinking about it."

Jake leaned around the tree trunk and stared into my face, with one of his black eyebrows raised. "Um, Faith, what's 'it'?"

"'It' is Gessert. Think about Gessert. No, no, wait a minute." I flapped my fingers in front of my mouth to erase what I'd said. "No, don't do that. Yes, do that, only first imagine a big, white ball above your head."

"How far above my head?"

I pointed to the gray sky. "Way up there. Since white

has all the colors, I see it as a sparkling huge ball. Sort of twinkling like a million prisms."

Jake nodded. "Got it. A big white ball way up there, and . . . ?"

"Then bring a ribbon of white down through the top of your head. . . . No, no, wait a minute. First you better get grounded."

"Grounded. Sure." He scooted around in front of me. "Faith, let's start with Roman numeral one. Is 'grounded' Roman numeral one?"

"Yes."

"And what's 'grounded' mean?"

"Well, that means that you're grounded. You're tied to the ground."

"So I don't fly up to the ball in the sky?" He had both eyebrows raised, and I felt a thump of disappointment. I had thought he'd take it seriously. Just like you do, Phillip. I must have looked discouraged, because he reached out and touched my chin with his finger. The things he said next he said in a solemn voice. "I want to do this with you, Faith, but you've got to get it together a little bit better. Now, explain how to get grounded."

I was thinking that I had been presenting everything in a scrabbly manner. I mentally picked through the different things Madalyn had taught us over the years. I decided on grounding, the white light, and breathing. And dead arms. That should get Jake prepared.

"Roman numeral one. Grounding. You imagine a cord coming out of the bottom of your spinal column and going down to the center of the earth." I sat up straight and felt the cord go from my spine to the center of the earth. Jake sat up straight, and I figured he was doing the same. "Roman numeral two . . .

"Oh-oh. I better explain that some people get visions, and some people get words, and some people get feelings. What we're going to do is ask a question, a very clear, precise question, and wait for an answer. The answer comes in different ways for different people. But the point of what we're going to do first is to be sure we don't give ourselves the answer."

Jake tilted his head forward so his black eyes were staring into mine. "Who gives us the answer?"

"I don't know. I asked my sister Madalyn, and she said maybe cosmic consciousness or maybe the collective unconscious. That's everybody's intelligence together, I think. Or maybe angels or guides. My twin brother, Phillip, asked Madalyn's friend Roger who gave us the answers, and he said, 'That's a good question.' "

Jake leaned back. "OK, Roman numeral two."

"Next you see the white ball and bring down a ribbon of white. . . . Oh, I'm sorry. Let's think of the question first. And then we can just go into the rest. My question is: Why is Gessert stealing coins?"

"What makes you sure he is?"

"I'm sure. Or I think I am. But if you don't want to ask a question, you could just say Gessert's name three times and see what impression you get. And then you can make your own deductions."

"Sounds fair. I'll do that."

I leaned against the tree again, and Jake bumped along the ground to his place behind me. "See the white ball above your head," I said in an imitation of Madalyn's soft voice, "and bring a ribbon of the white light down through the top of your head and through every part of your body and out the soles of your feet and back up to the white ball. Let the white light spread out from your body until it fills the space around you.

"Now pay attention to your breathing. Count your breaths as you exhale. Count them to ten. Then start back on one and count your exhales to ten again. Do this until you can't feel your arms, until you really can't tell if your hands are in your lap or on the ground. Then ask your question or say Gessert's name three times. Then keep paying attention to your breathing and wait."

I don't know how long it takes you, Phillip, but it takes me about ten minutes until my arms feel they're part of the air around me. As I counted my breaths, I heard Jake mumble, "William B. Gessert. William B. Gessert. William B. Gessert."

After a few more minutes of breathing, I forgot about Jake and let my question come up. "Why is Gessert stealing chains and coins?"

I saw the word *exchange*. Next came the word *melt*. Below that came the word *greedy*. I opened my eyes and waited for Jake.

"You done?" he asked.

"Yes."

He scooted around in front of me again. "What did you get?"

"I got the words *exchange, melt, greedy.* What did you get?"

"I didn't see or hear anything. I just thought of Gessert swinging his cane down the school hall, barking out a laugh when he was telling about the Donner party's dead baby, grabbing you after you cringed from his flying cane, and making fun of your drawings." Jake was silent a moment, his spacy eyes looking inward. "I don't believe that man has feelings for anybody but himself."

Phillip, do you think my words are right? Do you think Gessert would really melt down an ancient Spanish chain? I can't imagine a history teacher doing that. But I got the chills when Jake said Gessert had feelings for no one but himself, so maybe he'd do it.

Before he left, Jake said he'd had an interesting time. But the whole thing made me even more nervous about Gessert than I was before.

Your jumpy twin,
Faith

91

April 25

Faith,

Only an idiot would ruin that gold chain. It's worth a lot more as an artifact. Gessert probably didn't take it anyway. How could he have broken into the van in broad daylight without anybody seeing him? Especially since classes were almost out and there were bound to be some kids poking around. If Rex stole the gold, he could terrorize the kids into keeping their mouths shut. He suddenly came up with the money to throw that party last month, too.

Today Rex and my traveling as Soul really stirred things up. I'll start from the beginning.

Last night we had vegetable stew and I ate quite a bit.

In the middle of the night I threw up. Cynthia heard me puking and came into the bathroom. In between heaves, I asked her if there was any meat in the stew. She said, "No, no, I didn't put any meat in it, just a little soup-bone stock."

Real sweet. The ton of onions she put in the stew must have covered up the taste of dead animals.

When Howard woke me up in the morning to go to school, I told him I was too sick. In the afternoon, I listened to the Current of Sound and fell back asleep, silently repeating *Hu*. Next thing I know, I'm above my poisoned body.

I looked at the maple tree outside my window and was there. The fresh, little maple leaves had just sprung open. I marveled at how delicate and intricate they were, stretching for the sun. I turned my attention to the sky. It was full of drifting, cotton-puff clouds.

Suddenly I was among them. The speed with which this occurred startled me. I remembered what the man at Green Lake said about anchor points and used the clouds. I zipped from one cotton puff to another, a little jerkily at first, then smoother as I practiced. Wherever I put my attention, I would instantly be.

I was experiencing an incredible clarity, aware of every detail: The wisps of water vapor I passed through. Distant clouds illuminated against the blue sky. Even the city of Seattle bustling below was fascinating.

This soaring was such a rush. It felt like there were

millions of butterflies inside, all of them flying and me being swept along. The higher I flew, the better I felt. I saw a cloud above the rest and went for it, bursting with joy when I arrived.

The top was perfectly level, caused by two air masses of different temperatures. I wondered how I had sensed this and looked down at my body. I didn't have one! I looked closer and tried to see my arms. They began to materialize, but I drifted toward the ground.

It was a bummer because the beautiful, light, airy feeling I'd had had disappeared. So I bagged my arms and began floating back into the sky. I looked down and was surprised to discover Jefferson Junior High right below me.

Snap! Now I was in front of Jefferson and kids were pouring out. School must have just gotten over. Roxanne and Anthony were coming down the steps right at me. Roxanne must have asked him about his book again, because Anthony was telling her that he might let her read it next year. It was weird watching and listening to them. They had no idea I was even there.

Anthony said good-bye and they split up. I got the urge to follow Roxanne and did from tree-top level, feeling like a Peeping Tom. She was reading a book as she walked. I watched her approach Washington High, and I thought she would go around, but she surprised me by taking the shortcut. Good book, I guess.

Just before she got inside the courtyard, I saw him. Rex. He was standing out of her view, behind the corner of one of the buildings. I had no way to warn her. He stepped out between the two buildings she had to pass through.

"What's happening, Roxanne?"

"Rex! What are you doing here?" Startled, she closed the book.

Rex swaggered toward her. "I thought if I waited long enough, we could get to know each other."

"I've told you I'm not interested." Roxanne was trying to be hard-core. I knew it wasn't going to work this time. Even from where I was, I could see his hungry eyes. I checked to see if anybody else was around. Deserted.

"Come on, Roxanne. Don't tell me you'd rather be with the country worm." He was standing right in front of her.

"Get out of my way, Rex."

"Roxanne, what's the matter? You don't like me? Is that why you're always making a fool out of me in front of everybody?"

"Leave me alone."

"No way." He grabbed her. "I want you, *now*."

Roxanne screamed and I became aware in my body.

Leaping out of bed, I jerked my pants on and ran down the stairs. Cynthia was sitting at the dining room table as I picked up the phone. While dialing 911, I heard her say, "Phillip! What are you doing?"

A lady came on the line. "Can I help you?"

"I need the police."

"City, county, or state?" she asked.

Cynthia latched onto my arm. "Why are you calling the police?"

I tried to think. "Either city or county."

The lady made another attempt. "Sir, where are you?"

"Seattle," I replied.

"One moment, please."

"Phillip, what is going on?" Cynthia demanded.

I ignored her.

"Seattle Police Department," stated a man with a low voice.

"A girl is being assaulted at Washington High School," I blurted.

"Your name, please?" he asked.

"A girl is being assaulted right now!" I shouted. "Get somebody there."

"Your *name*," he asked again.

Cynthia tried to take the phone. "Give it to me, Phillip."

I pushed her away and hollered, "Cynthia, leave me alone!" She backed up and stood there, stunned.

"My name is Phillip O'Keefe," I told him.

"Where are you?"

"I'm at 643 . . ."

Cynthia recovered. "Officer," she yelled, "don't listen to him. He's been sick."

"What is going on?" he said, irritated.

"Believe me, a girl is being attacked right this moment at Washington High. Her name is Roxanne. The attacker is a guy named Rex."

"How do you know?"

"I saw it." The seriousness in my voice must have got

to him, because he quickly took my address and phone number, then told me he'd send a car right away.

I hung up, turned around, and faced Cynthia, who was glaring at me, mad as could be.

"Go to your room," she said in an icy voice.

I went.

About an hour later, I heard a knock at the front door, the door open, and a man say, "Is Phillip O'Keefe here?"

Cynthia replied, "Yes, he is."

"May I come in, ma'am?"

"Of course," she said. "I want you to know Phillip hasn't been feeling well lately."

I came down the stairs, not able even to imagine what was going to happen now.

"Hello, I'm Sergeant Peterson." His handshake let me know he was in control. "I'd like to ask you a few questions. Could we sit down?"

"Sure," I replied, surprised he wasn't in uniform.

"First, I'd like to know if you have been here all day."

What could I say? It would be a lie if I said yes. And if I said no, how could I explain? I told him, "Pretty much."

He leaned forward, "What do you mean, 'pretty much'?"

Cynthia cut in, "He's been here all day, Sergeant, and I've been with him."

"Let's get something straight. Phillip, you told the officer on the phone you saw a girl being attacked by a boy named Rex."

I had to know. "Did you stop him? Is she okay?"

"We arrested him, and she's fine. Now it's obvious to me that with the time and distances involved, you could not possibly have seen the assault. Who told you?"

"Nobody," I said.

"A friend didn't call and tell you?" He looked at Cynthia. She shook her head no. "Did Rex tell you he was going to do it?"

"No," I said.

"Look, I need a witness. Start talking."

"I saw Rex attack Roxanne while traveling out of my body."

Cynthia looked like she was going to have a heart attack. Sergeant Peterson swung around. "Has your son ever had any trouble with the police?"

"He's not my son," she replied. "He's a foster child and I don't know."

"Excuse me a minute." He got up and went outside.

I was relieved the police had saved Roxanne. When I looked over at Cynthia, I could see she was anything but relieved.

When Sergeant Peterson came back in, he told me, "Your record's clean, Phillip, but I don't buy this crap. If you want to help Roxanne, tell me the truth."

"I'm telling you the truth."

"Write it down." He handed me a form, then turned to Cynthia. "With your permission?"

She nodded yes.

I filled out the whole statement, and after Sergeant Peterson left with it, Cynthia sent me back up to my room.

When Howard came home, I heard Cynthia talking to him quietly. At dinner, neither of them said a word to me. I still felt queasy. After I finished picking at my plate, Howard told me to go back up to my room.

I cannot believe this happened, Faith. I gotta go to bed. Not feeling too well.

Friday night

I felt better and went to school today. Sergeant Peterson came and talked to the principal. I got called in and had to go through the whole story again in front of both of them. The principal told Sergeant Peterson that Rex and I are definitely not friends. And get this, the principal's door was open a bit, and the office assistant overheard and spread it all over the school.

When I walked into the lunchroom and saw Rex, I freaked. One look from him, and I knew he knew. Right then, Roxanne came up to me and gave me a big hug in front of everybody. "The cops told me you called them. The whole school is saying you were out of your body when you saw Rex attacking me. Were you?"

Embarrassed, and in front of the whole lunchroom, I said, "Yes."

Roxanne had a purple bruise on one cheek, but other than that, she seemed to be okay. She led me over to a table and we sat down. I was dying to know what happened after I went back to my body. "What did he do?" I asked.

"He didn't do or get anything. I fought like a cat. Look at him."

I turned my head and she was right. He had scratches all over his neck and ears. Rex saw me watching him, got up, and came toward us.

He was really mad. "What do we got here? A country worm that thinks it's a guardian angel."

I thought Roxanne would be scared. She wasn't. She was furious. "Get out of here, Rex. The cops told you to stay away, so book or I'll start screaming."

Rex didn't look at her. Just kept staring me down. Then he said, "You're dead meat," and left.

Suddenly I lost my appetite. I asked Roxanne if she wanted to skip lunch and go to the library.

In the library, Roxanne asked me, "How come you didn't tell me you were into out-of-body?"

From her expression, I knew she was a little hurt. "I used to astral-project, but got into trouble one night. The same thing could have happened to you if I encouraged it. Since then I've learned . . ."

Roxanne gave me a funny look. "You learned what?"

She was sitting across the library table from me with her back to the wall. I remembered what the teacher said. I knew it was okay to tell her. She would want to know how to travel as Soul.

"You learned what, Phillip?" she asked again.

I turned around to see if anybody could hear us. Nobody was close by.

"How come you won't tell me what you were gonna say?" she persisted.

"I will. I had to make sure we were alone and everything was cool. I need to be careful who I tell about this."

"Why's it matter?" she said. "The cops and everybody else in this school know about you."

"They only know a little bit," I replied. "Will you keep quiet if I tell you?"

"No problem. I can keep my trap shut."

I believed her. She's probably better at it than I am.

"I've learned how to travel as Soul. It's different from astral projection. It's finer and a lot more fun. In fact, it's totally shining."

I told her about the dream I had and the man at Green Lake. She couldn't understand why I hadn't asked him who he was. Before I could explain, the bell rang.

We left the library and went down to my locker. Before leaving for class, I lent her the copy of *In My Soul I Am Free*, which the man at Green Lake had given me.

After school, I came home to find Howard's pickup parked out front. I walked in the door, and there were Howard and Cynthia sitting in the dining room with all of my Edgar Cayce and astral projection books on the table.

Howard pulled a chair out for me to sit on. "Today I left Todd Shipyards early, Phillip. Do you know why?"

I knew perfectly well but said, "No."

"I came home to help you. I called Sergeant Peterson

after he had been to your school. He thinks you astral-projected. He doesn't see any other explanation for what happened and believes you're telling the truth. Needless to say, he will not be using you as a witness against Rex."

I probably should have kept my mouth shut, but instead said, "I wasn't astral-projecting."

"Oh, I know," he replied, like he understood perfectly.

That kind of threw me, and I wondered what he really did know. I sat there watching him for a few seconds, and then my gaze focused on the books. It pissed me off that he had taken them out of the oak desk. "You had no right to break into the desk and take these books."

Howard flared up, "I didn't break into the desk. I found the other key about a week ago, and Cynthia told me you tried to hide this book from her." He held up the astral projection book she had seen. "And I *do* have the right to know what you do and what you read. I am responsible for you and support you."

"You're not supporting me," I countered. "You get paid for taking care of me."

He slammed his hand on the table. "It's none of your business where the money comes from. I take care of you, and now you will listen. I don't see this the way you see it. And I don't see it the way the sergeant sees it. I see the truth."

I stopped him. "I'm telling the truth."

"Do not say one more word," he commanded. "You

103

may think it's the truth, but you have gotten lost. That is plain to see from what has happened and the books you are reading.

"I want you to come home directly after school from now on. The phone is completely off limits, no matter what the reason. You will come to our group meeting the Sunday after this coming one, and we will get you some help. Now go up to your room until we call you for dinner."

I got up to leave but then asked, "What about my books?"

In a fatherly voice, he replied, "I will keep these books. You won't need them anymore."

I wanted to argue, but it was obvious he wasn't going to change his mind. Man, Faith, the guy is totally out of it. I'm so bummed out, I wrote a letter to Roger telling him everything and hid it in my homework. Thanks for passing along his letter.

It looks like I'm going to be shut in for a while. Things might get a bit lonely.

Wish we could be together,
Phillip

PS. It's Saturday. My caseworker, Mrs. Langstrom, came by again this morning. (She came by last month, too.) Howard and Cynthia were both home. Mrs. Langstrom talked to all of us together. I was going to mention something about getting grounded, but after getting a piercing look from Howard, I kept my mouth shut. Unfortunately, she seems pretty satisfied with the way things are. On her way out, she told Howard she would just give him a call on the phone next month.

May 4

Dear Phillip,

I can't understand why your foster parents weren't at least relieved that you'd saved Roxanne, even if they didn't approve of how you did it. You haven't told me the name of their group, but Howard's actions don't sound like brotherly love to me. And I can't help you get away from him. Aunt Linda wouldn't take you now, even if she didn't have the excuse of having only two bedrooms. She thinks I'm awful, too.

I blew it last night after Linda went off to her Friday Bingo game. I was sitting at the dining room table drawing a slug I found in the garden. Since Mrs. Thompson gave me an A on my project and wrote on my paper that she thought I should consider being a wildlife or medical illustrator, I've been drawing every moving thing I can catch.

I was totally concentrating on my work when I heard a tapping. I looked up and saw Jake standing on tiptoe in the shrubs, peering through the window. I laughed and let him in.

After I'd salted down the slug and dumped it in the kitchen garbage can, Jake and I had a couple of Pepsis (bought with my own earnings), and then went into the "what do you want to do, play a game or watch TV, I don't care, what do you want to do." There was nothing good on TV. Jake decided he'd like to see what Gessert was up to.

It was still light out as we trudged around the lake and up the hill to Frontier Village. "There's his apartment," I said as we rounded the corner of his street.

"And there's Gessert!" Jake and I zipped behind a truck parked at the curb. We watched as Gessert shifted his cane to his left hand, searched for keys in his pants pocket, and unlocked the door of his convertible.

Jake leaned over the rear end of the truck. "What's that black and red thing he's got stuffed in his pocket?"

"That's a ski mask," I said and sat down on the pavement with a thump.

It was a long walk back to the Lake Stevens beach. The sky was dark when we arrived. "Let's rest on the bench," I suggested. "I'm beat."

The shadowy mounds of the sleeping ducks stretched

out and wobbled away from our feet as we settled down. "The moon isn't out tonight," Jake said.

"Yes, but there's the Big Dipper. I love it when it's dry. I hope it doesn't rain for a while. I hope we have a hot summer. I'd like to go swimming every day."

Jake bent down, picked up pebbles, and tossed them in front of us. They made *plop, plop* sound as they hit the water. "You'd better swim in the Pilchuck River instead of the lake," he said. "No duck shit."

It was getting late, I knew. I rose to finish the hike to Aunt Linda's, but Jake took my hand. "Nobody can see us here. Let's find out what Gessert's doing right now. I wanna try the remote viewing I read about in *Mind Race*."

So we sat together on the bench in the dark, meditating. As I concentrated on Gessert, I got the impression of his dark eyes being opened wide behind a mask. I asked the question "Why are Gessert's eyes opened wide?" and got the word *fear*.

"What'd you get?" I wanted to know when I felt Jake stir beside me.

"It was weird," he answered. "I thought I saw the inside of a store like a junk shop or pawnshop. It was dark, and I could barely make out a counter. Then everything was flooded with bright light, like somebody had flipped a switch on."

"I got Gessert with wide eyes and the word *fear*."

"Ha," Jake said, "he messed up this time."

"I hope he's caught."

"If he isn't, he'll beetle home and hide his car, I

bet. Let's walk back up and wait for him."

I stood up again. "I can't. It must be almost eleven now, and I gotta be home before Aunt Linda."

"Nuts," Jake said, getting up slowly beside me. "I'd like to find out if Gessert acts like he had a narrow escape, if he did escape."

I didn't blame Jake for wanting to follow up on his vision. When you first start practicing your little powers, you always want to check up to see if they're really real. I told him all this and said it was OK with me if he went back to Frontier Village alone.

"No, it would only be fun with you." He swung my hand in his as we walked along the beach road, and I almost forgot about my fear of Aunt Linda's beating me home until I saw her car parked in front of the house.

I stopped cold. "Oh, no, what am I going to do now?"

Jake didn't think it was any big deal. Jake doesn't know Aunt Linda. "Just walk in like nothing's the matter and tell her you've been up to Frontier Village with one of your junior high friends."

"Until eleven o'clock! I didn't leave her any note. I didn't tell her I was going out. She'll kill me." I was wiggling on one leg and then the other. I hadn't peed for three hours, and being scared was making it worse.

"Does she check your room when she comes home?" Jake asked calmly. Jake's always calm. I remember at Whidbey I used to think you were always calm, Phillip. I guess that's easier when your life is easy, but I never managed it even then.

"Well, does she check your room to see if you're there when she comes home?" Jake persisted.

"No, I don't think so. No. Whoa, the window! I always leave it open a bit." I silently eased over the grass and through the shrubbery to the side of the house. Jake was right behind me.

"It's open," I whispered, "but how am I going to climb in?"

"I'll lift you," he whispered back.

He boosted me up by my thighs, and I scrabbled for a good hold on the sill while I edged the window up with my head. Jake gave a final shove that sent me through the opening and head first onto the floor of the dark room. I got up on my knees to lean out and say good-bye when the light clicked on.

"What's going on in here?" Aunt Linda demanded.

"I . . . a . . . I . . . a . . ." I bet my eyes were wider than Gessert's. "I have to go to the bathroom."

Peeing gave me time to think; only I couldn't think of anything. She was waiting in the hall when I came out. "Get in there!" She jerked her head toward the living room, and I followed her meekly.

She stood in the middle of the rug with her hands on her hips and her eyes blazing. "Who was that boy?"

"It's Jake Krakowski. He's a friend from junior high. We went up to Frontier . . ."

"I don't want to hear any lies. Nothing's open in Frontier Village at eleven o'clock except Safeway."

"I know, but afterwards we were sitting down at the

beach. . . ." My voice dribbled away as her jaw clenched. I should have left the beach part off.

She took a step toward me. "You listen, young lady. I'm not going to have any little chippy in my house. If this ever, ever happens again, you'll be in a home for delinquent girls so fast it will make your head swim. Now go to bed!"

I did, fast.

I'd never heard the word "chippy" before, Phillip, but I think I've got the general idea of what it means. No use explaining and explaining I'm not one. Who believes us?

Faith

May 15

Dear Phillip,

What's happening??? It's been three weeks since I've heard from you. Worrying about you, feeling miserable about Aunt Linda, and not knowing what to do about Gessert has me living on the edge.

I've been wandering around the house for an hour propelled by guilt and indecision. Aunt Linda will be home from work in thirty minutes. I've made coleslaw and creamed chipped beef, which she likes, and put big potatoes in the oven to bake. I can't think of anything else to do for her.

When she bought me all those clothes, things were so

fun between us. I think she was beginning to like having me. Since I ruined everything by trying to sneak in the window, the only time she speaks to me now is when she has to.

I don't think of myself as a sneaky person. Mostly, I am an honest person. Partly because Mom said if we told on ourselves, we wouldn't get punished, which made it easy to get in the habit of telling the truth.

I would tell the truth about Gessert if I was positive I was right. And if I thought anybody would believe me. I really don't want anyone to get hurt because I'm chicken. I have to stop squirming around!

I looked in the *Seattle Times* Sunday, but there was nothing about a pawnshop robbery. When I got to school Monday, there he was, swinging his cane down the hall as if he were the duke of the place. During English (when I was supposed to be reading *Great Expectations*), I carefully went over what Jake and I got when we meditated. Wide eyes and fear didn't necessarily mean Gessert got caught in a pawnshop. All morning I was thinking maybe we had it figured wrong—until Jake came over to my table at lunchtime.

He dropped a newspaper clipping beside my tray. "How about *this*?"

The headline read: *Masked Robber Eludes Pawnbroker*. I whipped around to face Jake. "Where did you get it?"

He was looking down at me, grinning. "Sunday's *Everett Herald*. Gessert must be working closer to home."

"What's that? What's that about Mr. G.?" Sue Ellen

leaned across the table and snatched at the clipping.

Jake whipped it off the table. "Nothing for your eyes."

She pursed her lips indignantly. "We take the *Herald*. I can find out for myself."

"Good luck," he told her. He tapped me lightly on my head. "I'll see you after school, teacher."

When Jake left, Sue Ellen asked me, "Why did he call you 'teacher'?"

"Oh, because I taught him how to do something." I could see by Sue Ellen's gleaming eyes that she was ready to get her revenge by turning my remark into something nasty, so I gathered up my books and purse. I hated to dump my cherry cobbler in the garbage can, but losing it was better than listening to Sue Ellen.

On the way home from school, I tried to convince Jake that we should warn somebody that Gessert was the masked robber. Jake said we didn't have any believable evidence. He's right, of course. Nobody would have believed you, Phillip, if they hadn't caught Rex in the middle of attacking Roxanne.

But what if Gessert kills somebody with his cane?

If he does that, and I haven't told, my head will burst with guilt.

Faith

PS. *What* happened at the Group!!?

May 26

Faith

I'm sorry I waited so long to write. It's just that I've been in limbo myself until now. Howard has kept me practically imprisoned since the beginning of May, waiting to appear before the Group.

Every week I expected to go that coming Sunday. Then at the last minute, the meeting would get canceled. He never even said why. Only that the leader, a man named Mr. Cranston, was still in Hawaii. It drove me nuts.

Finally this morning, Howard woke me up and told me to take a shower and put my good clothes on. I didn't give him any crap. Next to the big macho pipe fitter from

Todd Shipyards, I'm just a scrawny little peon.

At breakfast table I was really beginning to feel desperate. I took a few small bites of my scrambled eggs, then said, "I don't feel very good. May I leave the table?"

Cynthia looked at me. "What's the matter? Is it your stomach?"

I was making myself appear as miserable as possible. "No, I've been hot since I got up."

Out of the corner of my eye, I could see Howard carefully watching me from his end of the table. "Take his temperature, Cynthia."

She scooted her chair back and left. I stood up and started to walk out of the dining room.

"Where are you going?" Howard wanted to know.

I kept on moving and replied, "I have to go to the bathroom."

I went inside and sat down on the pot to wait. After a bit, Cynthia knocked on the door and said, "Phillip, what are you doing? I've got the thermometer."

"I'm on the toilet. Just open the door and put it on the counter. I can reach it and take my temperature while I'm sitting here."

"Well, OK," she said hesitantly. "Make sure and stick it way back under your tongue."

I watched the door open and her hand slip in to lay the thermometer by the sink. After she closed the bathroom door, I stood up and got it. I figured if I used hot water, Howard would hear it running. Instead, I climbed up on

118

top of the counter and held the thermometer next to the light bulb.

Suddenly the door opened and there was Howard. "What is with you?" He grabbed my arm and pulled me off the counter. "Nobody is going to hurt you. I'm taking you to see Mr. Cranston because he is the only person I know who can help." He gave me a little shove out of the bathroom and let go of my arm. "Now get your clothes on. We're leaving in twenty minutes."

As we drove through the rain, Howard laid down some rules. The whole time, I just stared out of the window, his words landing on me like the drizzle falling on the street.

"When we get there, I want you to treat everybody with courtesy. When a man offers you his hand, take it smiling and introduce yourself. Don't make any smart-aleck remarks and don't try any tricks.

"Make me proud of you, Phillip. Mr. Cranston is a very important man. Be honored he has agreed to talk with you."

Howard guided the car into the driveway of a two-story gray house. I had been expecting a fancy building and asked him, "Is this it?"

"We have no place of our own yet. Those of us with larger homes trade off hosting the meetings."

The three of us got out of the car and began walking toward the front door. Cynthia touched my shoulder and said, "Let me straighten your tie. It's crooked." I let her do it while we waited for someone to answer the door.

It was opened by a fairly young man, probably in his early thirties. "Glad to see you." He pumped Howard's hand vigorously.

Howard stepped to the side and introduced me. "Mr. Cranston, this is Phillip. Phillip, this is Mr. Cranston."

I took his hand and had just about every bone in mine crushed. Quite the surprise. Howard and Cynthia had me expecting an old man in black, wearing glasses. Mr. Cranston was vibrant, had blond hair a little over his ears, no glasses, and was wearing a cream-colored suit.

He looked right at me, smiling. "How's it going, Phillip? I hear you've been having a bit of excitement." He kept ahold of my hand and guided me right through the door.

I didn't know what to say, so I didn't say anything.

"Let me take your jacket. Yours, too, Howard."

The room we were in had rows of folding chairs facing one wall. Against that wall was a table. Between the table and front row of chairs was plenty of room for someone to stand.

Howard and Cynthia began looking for a seat. I started to follow, but Mr. Cranston grasped my arm and said, "My assistant will be leading today. Let's go downstairs and get to know each other."

He brought me to a room that had a large black desk in the middle with a swivel chair behind it and a stuffed chair in front. He took the swivel.

Leaning back, he said, "Howard told me you saw a girl being assaulted while out of your body."

I kept quiet.

"I'll tell you what. I know Howard's a bit traditional. He's probably got you all freaked out. Let's make a deal. Neither one of us will let anything said in this room get beyond these walls. What do you say?"

"That sounds okay," I answered.

"Would you like to hear a little of my story?"

"Sure," I replied.

"When I was younger, I used to take drugs. Mostly psychedelics." He put his feet up on the desk. "I was always searching for that ultimate high. Always going for just a little more. Instead of ending up on top, I landed on the bottom. By my mid-twenties, I was wasted away with no home or job."

"How did you feed yourself?" I sat forward.

"Mostly garbage dumpsters and charity. Sometimes when I wasn't looking or smelling too bad, I'd go sit in a restaurant and wait for someone to leave their plate unfinished. Then I'd walk up and ask them if I could have it."

"Did the restaurants let you do that?"

"Once in a while they'd kick me out. Anyway, one morning I woke up on some cardboard in a railroad yard. I'd been drinking rot-gut wine, and I couldn't even remember how I'd gotten there. Through my bleary eyes, I watched the other bums. Some were sleeping in the dirt, others were sitting on the rails staring into space, and one guy was wandering around talking to the air. I said to myself, 'I've really hit the bottom of the barrel,' and started crying."

I was beginning to feel for the guy. "What happened? How did you get out of it?"

Mr. Cranston kept on laying himself open. "I cried until the Lord gave me a vision. He showed me how I could lift myself out of the hole I was in, through helping feed and clothe others who were down and out.

"I cleaned myself up and got a job. Took every dime I could spare and spent it on food and clothing for the poor. When I gave someone a gift, I'd tell them they could side with me in serving the Lord, helping the unfortunate. A few followed, and then gradually people with money began joining the cause."

"How many years did this take?" I said, thinking he had sure come a long way.

He took his feet off the desk and started to stand up. "Oh, it took about five years till I could quit working and do this full time. Now I'm starting a new group in Hawaii and training an assistant to run this one. Do you want to go for a walk?"

"In the rain?"

"Wait right here. I'll go get an umbrella."

While Mr. Cranston was talking, I hadn't really noticed what was going on upstairs. They were singing. A moment later a man began hollering, and the rest of the people were yelling in reply. This happened over and over. I was unable to make any sense out of what was being said. But every so often, it sounded like they were all stamping their feet. I was beginning to get alarmed when Mr. Cranston came back into the room.

I asked him, "What are they doing up there?"

"They're having a lecture," Mr. Cranston replied.

"A lecture? What kind of a lecture?" At that moment, the whole house was shaking from the pounding of feet.

He answered while escorting me from the room and out the back door. "It's a little different from the kind of lectures you're used to."

Once we were on the street, I felt better. I had a real bad feeling about coming to this Group. But at that moment, I guessed it must have been my own paranoia. Mr. Cranston seemed like a pretty nice guy. In fact, I thought he really wanted to help people and believed he was.

Walking in the rain with Mr. Cranston, under that umbrella, reminded me of Whidbey and the times Dad used to take me out. Maybe it was because this was the first time since the crash that an adult had done anything with me.

When we came to a street that had big trees growing out of the sidewalk, Mr. Cranston put his arm around my shoulder. "Howard told me about you, Roxanne, and the police. I'd like to hear it from you. Better yet, I'd like to know how you learned to leave your body. I've done a little studying myself in the area of out-of-body phenomena. You don't have to tell me if you don't want to, but I'm interested."

I tilted my head and looked at him. He really appeared to be sincere, Faith. I opened up. I told Mr. Cranston about you, Roger, and Madalyn, learning how to astral-project, Mom and Dad's encouragement, and getting stuck in the lower regions of the astral plane at the Wangsleys. I even told him about sneaking out of the bathroom window to meet the man at Green Lake.

Every so often he would prompt me with questions like: "Did your parents know how to project?" "Who else knew about it?" "Do any of the other kids at school astral-project?"

I answered every question and then some. I thought he was really understanding what I was saying, until I tried to explain the difference between astral projection and traveling as Soul. It was as though he was listening, but nothing was getting past his ears.

When I finished telling him about Howard taking away my books, I asked him if he would help me get them back. He took some black gloves out of his coat pockets and began putting them on. "Do you know what is really going on, Phillip?"

The question caught me off guard. "What do you mean?"

"I mean, do you really know what you have been going through?"

"Yes," I said, "I just told you."

"Phillip, you're being deceived. Now hold it; hear me out. You haven't been flying out of your body. Out-of-body phenomena are an illusion. The devil has cast a spell over you."

I felt like I had been kicked in the stomach by a horse. He hadn't heard a thing I said. I asked him, "How can you say traveling as Soul is an illusion after I helped save Roxanne?"

"Demons brought you that information," he replied abruptly. "The devil threw a dream over you and sent his demons in."

"Why would the devil want to rescue somebody who was being hurt?" I was in a state of total shock.

"In order to trap you. He has tricked you into believing you are pursuing something that is good, when in fact it is a technique to draw you deeper into his web."

I stayed silent for a couple of minutes, trying to collect my thoughts. We had turned around and were heading back. I listened to the patter of rain on his umbrella while watching his feet plopping on the sidewalk.

He had never been out of his body. And here he was explaining to me all about it. That didn't make any sense.

"Telling me I haven't traveled as Soul is like me trying to tell you, you aren't on this street right now." I looked at him. "How can you say that?"

He stopped walking, "Have you ever had a dream that you thought was real, and then woke up to find out it was just a dream?"

"Yes, I have. But we both got out of bed this morning, and when I'm traveling, I'm more than awake."

"I don't think you are, and I'm in the position to know, since the Lord woke me up in the railroad yard. I can help you awaken, and then you will see you were nothing more than a peanut on the road, with the devil running all over you."

When he said that, I couldn't believe it. I was beginning to think there was no hope. "Mr. Cranston, please listen to me. I've been leaving my body since I was a little kid. I can tell the difference between when I'm dreaming and when I'm not.

"I've learned how to do it by lots of practice and other people helping me, like the man at Green Lake. Traveling's a skill, just like learning how to ride a bike. Anybody can do it. To say all this is nothing more than a spell woven by the devil is stupid."

I probably should have kept that last remark to myself because Mr. Cranston started talking really fast. "The man you met at Green Lake is an agent for the devil. The Lord doesn't use other people to teach us; he can come to us and show the way himself. Only the devil has to use agents."

I interrupted him, "What about angels?"

"The Lord used angels a long time ago but doesn't need them anymore."

"I don't believe that," I replied. "I think angels still exist. I'm not saying the guy at Green Lake is one. He's probably just someone like me, who is a lot further along."

That really got him, because then he said, "Phillip, you're worse off than I thought. Now you're comparing yourself with an agent of the devil. I'm willing to try and help you, but you're going to have to work hard to cast off his spell. And if you aren't willing to try, I can't help and I've got to warn others the devil has you."

That made me mad. "What! Now you're gonna tell people what I've told you?"

"I have to protect them," he said. "If you don't fight

the devil, then that makes you his agent. I serve the Lord. I can't have you running around infecting others."

"You promised to keep whatever we talked about secret."

He countered with, "We both promised not to reveal what was said back in that room downstairs. There was no agreement made concerning what went on out here."

"You tricked me!" I looked at him. His friendly appearance had vanished. I left the protection of his umbrella and started running. It surprised him, which gave me a good head start.

When he did catch me, he grabbed ahold of the back of my neck. "I can help you, Phillip. It might take some time, but I can help you."

Mr. Cranston kept his grip on my neck all the way back to the house. He put me in that same room downstairs, locked the door, and left. I heard him go up the stairs as I collapsed into the stuffed chair. I couldn't help it, tears rolled down my cheeks as I wondered why Mr. Cranston was doing this to me.

About an hour later, the door opened. It was Howard. He said one sentence, "Let's go, Phillip."

I have no idea what Mr. Cranston told Howard, but in the car, he let me know I would be going to the Group regularly.

When we got home, I went straight up to my room, fell on the bed, and watched the drizzle through the window. I was so bummed I lay there until after it had been dark awhile.

Now I'm sitting at the empty oak desk, writing to you. Cynthia just called me to dinner. The thought of going down there makes me cringe.

Phillip

June 3

Dear Phillip,

I can't believe those terrible people. I feel so bad for you. But maybe help is on the way. Aunt Linda received a letter from Roger today. She read it through twice at dinner while she was chewing on pieces of round steak. This gave me plenty of time to make out the names on the envelope.

"That's from Roger Clinton?" I asked, passing her the blueberry muffins I'd made.

"Yes." She thoughtfully buttered her muffin. "Phillip writes to you. Doesn't he get along with his foster parents?"

"They're mean to him," I said and told her how they kept you in your room with no phone calls or anything.

Aunt Linda's old-maidish, but she isn't cruel on purpose. She frowned as I told her more about your life with the Wangsleys. I hope I have her mind set so that she's on your side.

And, Phillip, I need somebody on my side now. Bad. It isn't about Aunt Linda. She seems to be over my stupid window-climbing act. It's about Gessert. I'm afraid he'll try to get even with me.

After I wrote you last, I worried and worried about what I should do about him until Jake finally said why didn't I confide in Mrs. Thompson, she's a neat lady. She *is* a neat lady. Even so, it took all my guts. I didn't think she'd say I was an agent of the devil like those awful people you're with, but it might be hard for Mrs. Thompson to believe Gessert's cane was a gun just because I got the words *bullet clip*.

Yesterday I waited around her room until the last kid left for home. I was staring at her bulletin board and chewing on my fingernails when she asked, "Did you want to talk to me, Faith?"

"Uh-huh." I eased over to where she was sitting at her desk. "If you have time."

She smiled up at me. "I have time. Pull up a chair."

I pulled up a chair and began pouring out everything in my usual jumbled way, talking too fast and starting with Gessert's wide eyes instead of his cane. Mrs. Thompson listened awhile and then said, "Let's have a cup of tea."

While she boiled water on her Bunsen burner, set out mugs, and found her box of Almond Sunshine herb tea in the cupboard, I sweated over what she was thinking. Did she believe me? Did she think I was crazy? When she'd settled back down in her chair and handed me my cup, she said, "Now, why don't you tell me about the first time you picked up that there was something unusual about Mr. Gessert's behavior."

I took a sip of the hot drink, took a big breath, and began the story of Sue Ellen's and my trip to Mr. Gessert's apartment. At the end of my tale, Mrs. Thompson asked, "And your aunt, what does she say about all this?"

"I never told her."

"Not about going up to Frontier Village in the night?"

"Well, yes, she found out about that," I admitted. "But she thought I was just out with a boy. Doing something bad."

Mrs. Thompson looked down at her tea, which she was swirling in her mug, and nodded to herself. "And your brother, Phillip, what do his foster parents think of his out-of-body experiences?"

"They think the devil's got him."

"Hmmm." She kept swirling her tea, not saying anything more.

I waited and waited. Another teacher stuck her head in the door, murmured, "Oh, you're busy, Ruth," and, to my relief, went away.

"The only thing you can do now, Faith," Mrs. Thompson said slowly, "is tell everything you've told me to Mr. Hartman."

"The principal?" I squeaked.

She reached out and patted my hand. "I'll talk to him a little bit first, so he won't think you're coming in because of a discipline problem."

"Couldn't *you* tell him everything? Mr. Gessert already hates me. What would he do if he found out I narked to the principal?" I had snatched my hand away from hers and was sitting back in my chair in a complete panic.

"I am positive Mr. Hartman will be tactful and won't put you in any danger." She tried on her sweet smile, which really didn't get through to me this time. "I'll ask him to call you into his office when he has some free time tomorrow. Telling him is the best thing for you to do."

I wasn't so sure. And I wasn't so sure all night as I tossed around in bed. I had wanted to confess to Mrs. Thompson, because she reminds me of Mother and I'm used to confessing to her. But Mr. Hartman was another thing.

At two in the morning, I got up to go to the bathroom. At four, I heard Mrs. Tibbets's rooster crow. It was about five when I drifted off to sleep.

I awoke to find Aunt Linda by my bed. "Faith, it's almost eight o'clock!"

I rolled out from under my covers and was on my feet before I remembered my meeting with Mr. Hartman. Oh, you can talk to him, you big baby, I told myself.

By the time I got to second period, though, my courage

was leaking away. I hardly had enough spit to soften my clarinet reed. *What* if the principal called me out of social studies? Then Mr. Gessert would know it was me who narked.

But the secretary's voice came over the P.A. in third-period algebra. "Mr. Jenkins, will you please send Faith O'Keefe to the office?"

My mouth went dry again as I sat in the hard office chair and tried to smile nonchalantly at the student monitors who were bringing in absent slips from the classrooms. When Mr. Hartman finally did open his door and say, "Faith?" I stumbled getting up, gave him a weak, apologetic smile, and followed him into his inner office like a puppy about to be spanked.

"Now," he said as he settled behind his desk, "I hear you're trying out ESP."

I nodded dumbly from my seat.

"And you've been seeing Mr. Gessert in your trances? Trances? Do you call them trances?"

"I guess you could," I mumbled.

"Hmm." He folded his fingers into a little tent on his desk. "What kind of grades do you get in Mr. Gessert's class?"

Oh-oh, I could see where this was going. "I got a B at the quarter. We haven't had any grades since."

"And do you get along with Mr. Gessert?"

"Well, I don't think he likes me much."

The principal looked straight at me when he asked his next question. "Why do you suppose that is?"

"I think it's because he knows I know his cane is a gun."
There, I did it. I said it.

The muscles in Mr. Hartman's lined face didn't shift a fraction of an inch. "And what makes you believe his cane is a gun?"

"Because . . . because I saw it in two pieces. When Sue Ellen and I went to his apartment to sell him band candy, he said he'd just glued it together. Then, when I viewed him later, his cane was apart and I got the words *bullet clip*."

Mr. Hartman leaned back in his chair, put his hands behind his head, and stared at me with his upper lip sucked down under his lower lip. I wasn't scared anymore. I was telling it like it was, and if he didn't believe me, he didn't have to.

He looked up at the ceiling and then back at me. "Has anybody else seen anything Mr. Gessert has done? I mean, really seen it."

That pissed me off a little bit. What's real? "Jake Krakowski saw him get in his car with a ski mask when we were watching him from behind a truck last Friday night." My voice was sharp, but I didn't care.

Mr. Hartman's voice was equally sharp. "What time was that?"

"Sometime between nine and ten."

Mr. Hartman seemed to think that over. "Anything else?"

I shook my head no.

He rose slowly from his chair. "I don't want to say I

don't believe you, young lady, but without more evidence, I doubt if the police could pay much attention to your story. And I don't know what I could do about it, either."

As he guided me to the door with the back of his hand, I twisted my head around to face him. "Couldn't you just look at his cane?"

"Well," he said, "I guess I could do that."

I left the office relieved. The relief didn't last long. I'd forgotten to ask Mr. Hartman not to say anything to Mr. Gessert about me.

At lunch, boys usually sit at one table and girls at another, but you can mix it up if you want to. When I had my food, I walked over to the ninth-grade boys' table and plunked my tray next to Jake's.

"Howdy," he said with one of his black eyebrows raised.

I sat down. "I've got to talk to you."

He nodded and gave me his complete attention like he does. He's such a neat guy, Phillip. If I can't be with you, he's next best. I told him everything that had happened with Mrs. Thompson and everything the principal had said.

Jake thought a minute when I was through. Then, after two more bites of his pizza, he said, "I guess all you can do now is wait to see if Hartman does anything."

Hartman did something. Right in the beginning of social studies. Jake and I exchanged quick glances as he came in our classroom door with the burly P.E. teacher behind him. Mr. Gessert slid off the edge of his desk and gave them a smile in greeting.

Mr. Hartman merely tipped his head. "I wonder if we could talk to you a minute?"

Mr. Gessert followed the principal and coach out of the room. In the hall, he stood facing them, holding the door ajar as if he were such a conscientious teacher that he had to keep one eye on his class. I scooted down in my seat and listened without breathing. I heard the word "cane." Gessert laughed and then said, "What's the matter? You got a gimpy athlete?" He was smooth! "I'm sorry, though, I didn't bring it today."

Mr. Gessert opened the door wider, and I saw the coach take a step back. Gessert was going to get away free. His cane was in the closet. Everybody in the class knew.

As he entered the room, Gessert shot a glance at me that was filled with so much venom my insides were seared with fear. The picture of the dead mallard rose in my head.

Jake stood up. "Wait a minute, Mr. Hartman! Wait a minute!"

Mr. Hartman hesitated in the hall. Gessert's eyes shifted to Jake. Oh, my God, Jake'd get it, too. I tried to say, "No, Jake, no," but my voice came out in little squeaks.

"Mr. Gessert's cane is in the closet. We all saw him put it there before class started." Jake was ignoring Gessert and looking straight at the principal, who'd come in from the hall followed by the coach.

"Oh, you're right, Jake. I forgot. I did bring it. It was my umbrella I decided I wouldn't need." Gessert moved toward the closet. "I'll get the cane for you."

"Never mind." Mr. Hartman brushed past him. "I can get it."

"It's under my raincoat there."

The P.E. teacher's gaze shifted to where Gessert was pointing, and at that instant Gessert slipped behind him and was out the door. The coach whirled and made a grab for Gessert. I didn't know that chunky man could move so fast. But it wasn't fast enough. Gessert was gone.

Miss Etham entered the classroom, holding some library slips. Mr. Hartman shoved the cane at her, told her, "Here, don't let this out of your sight," and dashed down the hall after the two teachers. Miss Etham stared at the cane, bewildered, and then tried to get the class in order, which was useless.

Some of the kids were poking their heads out the classroom door; the rest were at the windows. I was scrunched in my seat, saying over and over, "Please catch him. Please, please catch him."

"There he goes," shouted Ray, "in his silver bullet!"

The kids at the door rushed to the windows where Ray stood. Jake and I, who were the only ones seated, stared dismally at each other. Miss Etham, still holding the cane, pleaded with the kids to sit down.

It took her ten minutes to get the class settled into reading the next chapter in the social studies book. It was ten minutes later when Ray stretched up in his seat, peered out the windows, and announced, "The cops are here."

That was when the bell rang, ending the period. Jake and I left the room together, followed by dumb Sue Ellen, who was whining, "I don't see why they wanted to take poor Mr. G.'s cane away from him."

"I'd give anything to have poor Mr. G. in the slammer," I muttered to Jake.

He walked me down to science class, where I sat shivering while Mrs. Thompson lectured on genes. It was at the end of that period when I was called down to the office again. Mrs. Thompson came over to the door as I was leaving and whispered that she'd be in her room after school if I needed someone to talk to.

Two deputy sheriffs were with the principal. Mr. Hartman told me to sit down. There were a few questions that the officers wanted to ask me.

Mostly they quizzed me about Friday night. What time did I see Mr. Gessert leave in his car? What kind of a car was it? How close was I to him when I saw the ski mask? How did I know it was a ski mask he was carrying?

"I knew it was a ski mask, or I thought it was," I told them, "because I could see red yarn or a red outline around the eye holes. The top was hanging out of his pocket while he searched for his keys."

The deputies exchanged glances. The one who was writing everything I said on his clipboard asked, "What did you do after you saw the ski mask?"

"I sat down on the road behind the truck."

"Why did you do that?"

"Because I was scared." Why did he think I did it? I was still scared. Who was going to keep Gessert away from me?

Before I could ask *my* question, the deputy with the clipboard stood up, took a card from his wallet, and handed it to me. "You've been very helpful, Faith. If you pick up any more information about Gessert, please give us a call."

Mr. Hartman ushered me out the door again. Jake was sitting in the outer office. I tried to give him a little smile before the principal took him in to the police.

I was too freaked to talk to Mrs. Thompson. I came straight home to tell you what happened, Phillip. There's no way I can meditate and find out what Gessert's doing by myself. I can hardly sit still enough to write. I jump at every little sound and just keep thinking: He knows I narked. He knows I narked. Poor Jake. Gessert knows he narked, too.

Phillip, can you help me? Could you zero in on where he is? Since Jake saw him in his car, couldn't you use his gray Fiat convertible as a focus point?

Please try. Even though you're with those miserable people, try. Oh, I know you will. What's the matter with me? Only do it as soon as you receive this letter. I tried to call you long distance when I got in the house, but Mrs. Wangsley answered and said you couldn't have phone calls. What a witch!

I'll take this letter down to the Lake Stevens post office to get it in the five o'clock mail pickup. Hurry with your reply, Phillip. Call me if you get a chance. I'm petrified of that man.

Faith

June 5

Faith,

Why did they let him get away? The principal should have called the police. A teacher's got a gun in the classroom, and all he does is walk in and ask to see it? Gessert could have grabbed the cane instead of running.

He strikes me as the revengeful type. I wish I could call you up and give you some advice. Such as locking all the doors and windows. Or finding out if Aunt Linda has a gun. I feel helpless. I guess the best I can do is try to find him tonight before I go to sleep. Then send this letter tomorrow.

Gessert's my top suspect for the gold theft from Jefferson. Roxanne uncovered another piece of the puzzle today. We were heading home from school and were almost to her street when she touched my shoulder. "I was talking to Anthony in sixth period, and it came out he went to that party two months ago."

"The free one Rex had?"

"Yeah, but get this, Anthony went to the party and found out it was somebody else's."

I stopped walking. "You're kidding?"

"No, I'm not," she replied. "A friend of Rex's brother paid for it. The guy just got an inheritance from his grandfather and was celebrating."

"It's strange Rex went around talking that party up so much. He must have known people were going to find out he was lying."

Roxanne started moving down the street. "He just had to be a big shot."

When we reached Roxanne's house, she turned to me. "Come on in for a while."

My insides tingled. "You know I'm supposed to go straight home."

She took ahold of my hand and pulled on it. "Fifteen minutes won't hurt anything. My mother's been dying to meet you."

I hesitated for a moment longer, then tried to relax as I let her lead me into her house.

"Mom, I brought Phillip home. You want to meet him?"

I heard a door slam, and then a pretty, young woman

walked into the living room. She couldn't have been much over thirty, had the same blond hair as Roxanne, and was wearing blue jeans.

"Mom, this is Phillip O'Keefe. Phillip, this is my mother, Deseria DeBuque."

She held out her hand, and I took it, receiving a gentle handshake. Her vibes were really smooth. No wonder Roxanne is so neat.

Deseria let go of my hand. "I want to thank you for helping to save my daughter. Roxanne's told me how hard you've had it since then. I, for one, really appreciate what you did."

I was totally speechless.

Roxanne rescued me. "We're going upstairs to my room."

"Would you kids like something to eat?"

"Phillip can only stay for a minute," Roxanne said. "He's got to go home or he'll get in trouble. I was just gonna show him my parakeets."

Roxanne's room was full of plants, all healthy and spilling out of their planters. In one corner of the room was a huge homemade cage with two parakeets in it.

"Did you used to have more parakeets?" I asked.

"No, just these two. I want them to have lots of freedom. I can let them out, too. Here, watch." She opened the door, and the blue one came out and landed on her shoulder. The green one hesitated, then flew out and onto a redwood planter hanging from the ceiling.

I laughed. "It's a jungle in here. I bet they feel right at home."

"Do you like it?" she asked.

"I love it." I noticed there were skylights in the ceiling. "How do you get everything to grow so well?"

"I give my plants lots of love and tell them they can get as big as they want."

"It must work." I sat down on her bed.

Roxanne settled beside me with the parakeet. "I've been working on the traveling-as-Soul technique you told me about."

"You can hear the Current of Sound?"

"I've been able to hear a high-pitched tone inside my head since I was a little kid. Last night while practicing, I discovered a weird coincidence."

"What?" I asked.

"*Hu*-man," she replied, accenting "Hu."

"That's pretty wild. Listen to this. I looked up 'God' in the Oxford dictionary. It traces 'God' back to the word 'Hu.' "

Roxanne leaned back against her pillow. "Kind of makes you wonder, huh?"

"Yeah, it does." I spotted a clock on the wall. "I got to get going."

She took the parakeet off her shoulder and put it on a plant, saying to it, "I'll be right back."

On the way downstairs, Roxanne said, "The reason I left school early yesterday is because I went to court and testified against Rex. The judge ordered him to stay away from me."

"That's all?" I interrupted.

"No, as soon as school's out, he's got to start doing community work for the whole summer."

"What'd Rex think of that?"

"Not much."

Roxanne was opening the front door when her mother came into the living room. "I'm glad I got to meet you."

"Goodbye, Mrs. DeBuque."

"Just call me Des, Phillip. You're making me feel like an old woman."

"Okay, Des, see you later."

She smiled, and I stepped out onto the porch. Roxanne followed and closed the door behind her. "My mother's not a Mrs. She's never been married."

"Oh, I'm sorry."

"Don't be." She stepped closer to me. "I want to thank you right for rescuing me from Rex."

My face burned red.

She took my chin in both her hands and kissed me lightly on the lips. Pulling away, she said, "Bye," then spun around and went in the house.

I can tell you one thing, Faith, I was sparkling inside when I bounced off her porch and headed for the Wangsleys'.

Cynthia was in the kitchen when I came in the front door. A Seattle newspaper was lying on the dining room table. The bold headline of an article caught my eye. I read it and then copied it down for you. If I ripped it out, Howard would tweak.

TEACHER TURNS SCHOOL TREASURE
INTO OWN POT OF GOLD

A Spanish treasure of gold, stolen from Jefferson Junior High last February, has found its way into the pot of Lake Stevens Junior High teacher William B. Gessert.

The Snohomish County Sheriff's Office reported a student gave them a tip that resulted in the flight of Mr. Gessert from the school. A search of his apartment uncovered the one remaining piece, a gold chain. The chain was identified by underwater archaeologist Dr. James G. Rassmussen as belonging to the treasure.

Also found was an oxygen-acetylene torch and crucible. Officers speculate the rest of the treasure, in the form of gold coins, has been melted down in the crucible and sold.

One of the students at Lake Stevens Junior High reportedly used ESP to determine Mr. Gessert had converted a walking cane into a gun and was committing robberies. An investigation is now in progress to discover if the fugitive, William B. Gessert, is the person who has been robbing pawn and coin shops in the North End.

The article makes it sound like you said Mr. Gessert was holding up shops with his cane. They didn't get all of the facts straight, but at least your name was left out. Big help. Mr. Gessert will probably know you narked on him anyway.

I went to the Group last Sunday. It was held at the same house, and this time I sat with Howard and Cynthia. While we were waiting for the session to start, a black, padded box with silver tassels was being passed around. People were putting money in it. When it got to Howard, he put a wad of cash in it that included at least a couple of hundred-dollar bills. No wonder his house is falling apart.

First thing Mr. Cranston does when he gets up in front of everybody is introduce me. Like nobody knows who I am. I could tell by the "oh, such a poor lost soul" looks people were giving me, he had leaked our little conversation in the rain.

After he finished playing that game, Mr. Cranston gave a report on his progress in Hawaii. He rented a building while he was there. Next month some of his diehard followers are moving there with him to set up business. His assistant, a dark-skinned guy named Dixon, is staying here to run this group. Dixon, who was sitting behind Mr. Cranston on the edge of the table, looked rather pleased to hear the good news.

When Mr. Cranston had finished, Dixon took over. He led the Group in some songs after having everybody stand up. I stood but was too nervous to sing. He did a real good job, especially considering he was singing without any musical instruments.

The first line of one of the songs caught my attention: "Amazing grace, how sweet the sound, that saved a wretch like me."

It dawned on me that the songwriter was saying grace can be heard as sound. I was thinking about that and just starting to get calmed down, when all of a sudden a voice cried out, "There is one among you who is not with us! Put down your burden and pick up our yoke. For it is light and will guide you on the straight and narrow path."

Immediately, the whole crowd, including Howard and Cynthia, stopped singing, got down on their knees facing the rear of the room, and placed their heads on the seats of their chairs. Mr. Cranston and I were the only ones left standing. I sat down, but Mr. Cranston remained. He stayed at the front of the room with his eyes closed. Dixon was kneeling away from him, forehead touching the floor.

I looked around to see who was causing the commotion, but didn't have any luck.

"Let go of your load, forsake the devil, and come forth. Leave the fires of hell and let us lift you onto the way. To play with the devil is to invite death and destruction. To pick up our yoke is to embrace truth and righteousness."

On the last sentence I located the person doing the talking. Her head moved to the rhythm of her words. She was just a kid, probably in her late teens. I'd noticed her when I first got there because she was so much younger than the rest. Now she was kneeling in the front row. As she continued spouting off, I wondered why she was doing this to me.

"Come and spill your pain; let us replace it with love. For the road you travel now is littered with demons. They have blinded and deceived you. Turn around now before you are past the point of no return."

Mr. Cranston broke in. "You know who you are. Abandon the devil and come to the front of the room. Our love will shatter his bonds and awaken you. Do it now!"

He yelled this last statement, and everybody else started repeating it over and over. "Do it now! Do it now! Do it now! Do it now!" Each time they said it louder, building it up into an incredible crescendo. I could almost feel them pulling at me physically.

Now I was freaked. This was total insanity. I found myself thinking, What will they do to me if I don't go up there? The pressure and tension were getting so intense, it felt like the room was about ready to explode and I was about ready to run out of that house.

Then, as quickly as it started, it stopped. They all got up and sat down in their chairs, looking like one of their own had just died. Mr. Cranston wrapped it all up by staring right at me and saying, "Thank you all for coming. I'll see you next week."

Must have been the shortest meeting they ever had. As Cynthia, Howard, and I left, not one person would look at me.

Well, that's how I'll be spending my Sundays for a

while. I'm going to bed now and see if I can find Mr. Gessert.

Locating him was effortless. All I did was imagine I was looking at his car the moment I was past the brink of sleep. In a flash, with no trace of motion, I was there watching him drive by a great big white arch. I was confused until I noticed the Canadian and American flags flying together. It was the Peace Arch on the border between the United States and Canada.

As soon as I realized he was going into Canada, I put my attention on the feel of the covers against my skin and opened my eyes back in my bed. Thinking I could figure out where he was headed if I had a map, I pulled my pants on and went downstairs.

Howard and Cynthia were still awake. Howard looked up from the magazine he was reading and asked me, "What are you doing? I thought you went to bed."

"I was wondering if you had a map of Washington or British Columbia I could borrow."

"What for?"

I couldn't believe it. All I wanted to do was look at a map. I knew if I told him the truth, I'd never get to see one. And he'd probably make me hold books for a half an hour. "I'm working on a geography report for school."

He just stared at me for a second. "What's the report on?"

Talk about suspicious. I had to think quick. "It's about

the border towns between British Columbia and Washington."

Howard looked over at Cynthia. She was knitting, ignoring both of us. "Where did you put the map of British Columbia I gave you last week after cleaning out the car?"

She just kept on knitting and said, "In the kitchen in the junk drawer underneath the silverware."

Howard started reading his magazine again, so I went and got it.

Back upstairs, I spread the map out on my bed. Mr. Gessert was going into Canada at the big border crossing. That's the one near Blaine, Washington. Looking at the map, I can see Interstate 5 connects with Canadian Highway 99 there. So he was going north on 99, which leads to Vancouver. He could branch off and head east on Highway 1, but it's a long way to any big cities. I figure he'll go into Vancouver, where he can blend in better.

I love you very much,
Phillip

PS. It's Thursday and I'm in first period. We're supposed to be studying, but I'm adding to this letter instead.

This morning I had a dream I was back on Whidbey. You and Mom were weeding the garden. Madalyn was in the house making lunch, and Dad and I were working on the old tractor.

Someone started to call my name. Putting the wrench down I had in my hand, I stood up. When I turned around

151

to see who it was, I found myself in a void. A great, big empty space.

Far away I saw a light. I moved toward it, or it came closer to me, and I discovered it was the man from Green Lake. He looked exactly the same, except his body was made out of light.

He held out his arm. "Take my hand."

The instant I touched it, both of us were standing in the rain on a street. There were great big trees on the other side. Underneath them was a man with an umbrella and a kid. When they got closer, I was shocked to discover the man was Mr. Cranston.

He asked the kid, "So what did you do?"

"I snuck out the window and down to Green Lake."

I gasped. It was me! I turned and looked at the man next to me. His face was expressionless. I looked back at Mr. Cranston, who was talking. "Did the man show up?"

"Yeah, he did. He even gave me a book."

I watched and listened as Mr. Cranston pumped me and I responded, telling him everything. When the black gloves came out of Mr. Cranston's pocket, I knew what was going to happen next. If only I had thought about what I was doing.

After I saw myself shout, "You tricked me," and run into the rain, I opened my eyes in bed. I lay there, knowing I had blown it. Mr. Cranston was the way he was. If I had kept my mouth shut, things would be much better than they are now.

The alarm went off, so I got out of bed and went down

to breakfast. Beside my plate at the table was a letter addressed to me. It was already ripped open. I wondered who had done that, until I saw it was from Roger. Mr. Cranston must have told Howard and Cynthia about him.

I read the letter and was stunned. He wants to take you and me to the Caribbean this summer. My spirits soared until I looked up and found Cynthia watching me closely. It hit me. She and Howard are never going to let me go. Especially after what I told Mr. Cranston about Roger. There was no point in asking her why they opened my letter. I knew. I just got up from the breakfast table and left for school.

After my last class, I'm going to the post office to mail this letter and call you from the pay phone. If I get in trouble for being late, that's the way it goes. I want you to know there's nothing to worry about anymore, Faith. Gessert's in Canada.

PPS. Nobody answered.

June 8

Phillip!!!

You did it! You did it! You absolutely wonderful twin
brother, you. I've just called the cops, called Jake, and
then grabbed some paper to write you right away. I'm
supposed to be making a pie for company Aunt Linda's
having, but it can wait a few minutes. Anyway, I think
I've buttered (fattened?) her up enough trying to get back
in her good graces. This morning when she was dressing,
she yanked her skirt back off and swore at the cleaners
for shrinking it.

I did get myself together enough a couple nights ago to

visualize where Gessert was. I just got a vague impression of the outside of a white motel, though. There must be a hundred white motels in Washington, so I didn't bother to call the sheriff's office.

When I called them a few minutes ago, I had trouble getting your information across. Either the woman who answered was sleepy or she had never heard of the Peace Arch. "Your brother thinks this man's at a peace march?" she kept asking.

"He was driving *by* the Peace *Arch*," I kept explaining. "My brother saw Gessert in his gray Fiat convertible driving *by* the Peace Arch."

"Please hold the phone." She sounded as if she'd snapped awake. Maybe my mentioning the Fiat triggered her memory.

The deputy who had given me his card took the phone next. He was all business. "You can relax now," he said after I'd relayed your information. "We'll notify Canada, and if Gessert's in Vancouver, the Mounties should have him picked up shortly."

Maybe *he* thinks I can relax now, but I'll really relax when I *know* Gessert's in the slammer. Those cops blabbed more than you did. I wish your teacher-man would take them on a trip after they talk to the newspapers. Oops, it's about time for Aunt Linda to be home from grocery shopping, so I'd better get at the pie. I'll finish this letter before I go to bed.

Guess who came to dinner?? Roger! Oh, whoa, talk about being surprised. Aunt Linda stood around smiling while I hugged him and hugged him. He brought me pictures of the Spanish galleon he'd uncovered in the Caribbean. I wanted to hear about all his adventures in underwater archaeology, but he wanted to hear about all our adventures.

During dinner I told him the whole Gessert story. When I got to the part about Jake and me seeing the ski mask, Aunt Linda interrupted. "Faith, why didn't you tell me that's what you were doing in Frontier Village at night?"

"You gave me a chance?" I asked her. She colored a little at that. I think she likes to look cool in front of Roger. He was older than Madalyn, but Aunt Linda must be at least ten years older than he is. You wouldn't know it from the way she flutters around him.

She passed him some more baked chicken breasts, and I went on with my story. When I got to Gessert running out of the school, Roger's face turned solemn. But then I handed him your letter, and he read it and smiled. "You notified the police?" he asked.

"You bet," I said.

He turned to Aunt Linda. "Phillip seems pretty unhappy where he is."

Aunt Linda rushed to tell Roger how sorry she was about that, but she just had a little house with only two bedrooms, and she was a lone woman. . . .

Roger soothed her, saying he understood that it would be hard for her to take a boy, but . . .

And then Roger said—listen to *this,* Phillip—Roger said, ". . . but I'd like to become Phillip's foster parent."

I was so excited when I heard Roger say that, I bounced, bug-eyed, in my chair.

"Well," Aunt Linda said, putting down her forkful of chicken, "I think you would have to have suitable housing in the area."

"I have my condo in Seattle," Roger told her.

"Oh, then I'm sure you could take him. I'll be glad to do anything I can to help with the legalities."

Wowee! I pushed back my chair and was ready to dive for the phone and *make* that Mrs. Wangsley let you talk to me, when Roger went on. "After we get the foster parentage settled, I'd like to take both Faith and Phillip to Florida with me for the summer."

"I don't know," Aunt Linda said in a little voice. "Faith has her school here."

"It's June. School should be out soon. Right, Faith?"

I nodded, too full of hope to speak.

"We'd be coming back before school takes up again in September," Roger added.

Aunt Linda still looked doubtful, so I pleaded, "Please, Aunt Linda, please let me go. I miss Phillip so much. It isn't easy to be separated from a twin." My voice caught on the last word, and tears rolled down my face.

It was the first time I'd cried in front of Aunt Linda,

and it seemed to upset her. She put her napkin to her mouth, waiting a minute before she answered, "Well, let's see if we can arrange for Roger to have Phillip, and then we'll talk about the summer."

With Aunt Linda's help, I know Roger can yank you away from those Wangsleys, Phillip. The Caribbean! Lost treasures! You'll be flying all night searching for those sunken Spanish galleons.

When he left, I hugged Roger some more and whispered for him to tell you I'll be along on the trip. I will, even if I have to feed old Linda pies and cookies and muffins till her stomach bursts.

Faith

June 20

Roxanne,

I'm sorry we haven't been able to see each other since school ended. Without even knowing you, Howard says you're a bad influence.

You've been on my mind a lot. What stands out is how you always stick up for yourself. Even against Rex at Washington High. I think that's cool.

When I lived on Whidbey Island, I had plenty of friends. There were kids in our school who got picked on, but nobody bothered me. I came to Seattle, and suddenly I was the low man on the totem pole. I never learned how to take that.

Remember my Aunt Linda and Roger Clinton were going to talk to my caseworker? Well, they did. She came to the Wangsleys' this evening.

Howard took off early from the shipyards. He got all spruced up. Cynthia spent the whole day cleaning house. By the time my caseworker arrived, she had everything spic and span.

When a knock came at the door, Howard answered it with the grace of a butler. "How are you, Mrs. Langstrom? Please come in." He ushered her into the living room and onto the couch. Cynthia gracefully placed a tray of cookies and tea on the coffee table, then sat next to Howard and served us.

I was off to the side in an easy chair, watching the play. Howard spoke first. "Mrs. Langstrom, I understand Phillip's aunt has told you he's unhappy here."

She set her teacup on the table. "I'll get right to the point. Phillip's aunt believes he would be better off under the care of Roger Clinton. I had a meeting with Roger. He's willing to legally adopt Phillip. I understand that outside of his aunt, Phillip is closer to Roger than anyone else."

My heart leaped. Roger actually wants to adopt me? Then I stopped chewing my cookie and thought: Who told her that about my aunt? I hardly know Linda.

Howard crossed his legs. "Don't you think it would be preferable for Phillip to be living in a two-parent environment?"

"That's a good point."

Howard continued, "And Cynthia and I have decided we would like to adopt Phillip."

My caseworker leaned across Howard to look at Cynthia. Cynthia looked a little taken, but nodded her head obediently.

I just about choked. Trapped with the Wangsleys until I was eighteen would be more than I could stand.

My caseworker settled back. "In my opinion, the respect Roger Clinton commands in the community, and the fact that he's an old friend of the family, outweigh the single-parent issue. I guess what it comes down to is what do you want, Phillip?"

All heads swiveled to look at me. I focused on Howard, who was giving me a domineering glare. I stared back and said, "I'm being suffocated. I've had to come home right after school for months. Now that school's out, I'm hardly allowed to go anywhere. The phone's been off limits, and I haven't seen my twin sister, Faith, since I've been here. I can't take any more. I want out."

Cynthia's face turned pale. Howard's face was red with anger, and my caseworker appeared shocked. "Phillip, why didn't you tell me about this before?"

"I was chicken."

She regained her cool. "Well, that settles it. I'll pick Phillip up tomorrow at twelve o'clock. Could you have him ready?"

"I think you should reconsider," Howard said. "Phillip needs discipline."

"There are a lot of different methods of raising a child."

Howard was about ready to say something else, but before he could, Mrs. Langstom stood up with her purse. Cynthia started to rise. My caseworker stopped her. "Don't bother. I can let myself out." She went to the door and opened it. "Please have Phillip ready when I come to get him tomorrow. I'll be making arrangements with Roger Clinton. Good night."

After the door shut, Howard faced me. "You shouldn't have done that."

"I want my books, Howard."

"I don't have anything that belongs to you."

"You're lying. You took 'em, and now I want them back."

"The books you speak of belong to the devil. And I'll be damned if you'll ever get them." He jumped up. "Go to your room."

I walked out, came upstairs, and started writing you this letter. I look back and realize I should have said something to my caseworker a long time ago. You would have. Hopefully this will be my last night at the Wangsleys'. I'll believe it when I'm gone.

I'm gone.

The Canadians caught Mr. Gessert! I was sitting in the living room of Roger's condo watching TV when it came on the six o'clock news. There was even a shot of him being hustled into a car with handcuffs on. I bet my sister's relieved.

I'm having a shining time with Roger. It's only been a

day, but already the smothered feeling that was stuck on me at the Wangsleys' is beginning to peel off. It feels so good to be free again.

Leaving the Wangsleys' was a trip. Before my caseworker got there, I asked Howard for my books again. He tried to ignore me, but I told him, "Hand my books over. Otherwise I'm gonna tell my caseworker you stole them from me."

He put the newspaper down. "Don't threaten me. I'll tell Mrs. Langstrom I don't know what you are talking about."

She showed up right on time. I got all my stuff in her car and was ready to tell her when Cynthia scurried into the living room. "You almost forgot your books, Phillip."

"What are you doing, woman?" Howard tried to snatch them, but I got my hands on them first. Mrs. Langstrom stepped between us.

Howard grabbed Cynthia by the arm. "Have you lost your mind?"

"Let them go, Howard! They're poisoning us. Let them go."

My caseworker guided me outside, and we left to the sound of Howard shouting and Cynthia crying. I was so glad to be out of there, I hardly noticed. But later in Mrs. Langstrom's car, I thought about Cynthia. She had tried to be a good mother, putting up with my vegetarianism and all. You know, Roxanne, I feel like she was kind of swept along in what happened. Oh, well.

Now I'm just kicking back, free as a bird sitting at an

old teak table in Roger's dining room. His condo is perched on Queen Anne Hill, and in front of me is a spectacular view of Puget Sound. I'm so happy, I feel like I could fly right through this picture window and out over the water.

Roger and I are leaving in a few minutes for a dinner at Aunt Linda's. He's trying to talk her into letting Faith come to the Caribbean with us.

Part of me is really happy I'm going to the Caribbean, and part of me is sad. I'm gonna miss you, Roxanne. Thanks for being such a good friend and sticking up for me at Jefferson. Without you, Jefferson would have been pretty bleak, and I could still be back there at the Wangsleys', sniveling.

As soon as I know what it is, I'll write and give you my mailing address in the Caribbean.

My heart is with you,
Phillip

PS. How's the traveling as Soul going?

June 26

Dear Jake,

I tried to see you before I left, but your mom said you were on a fishing trip with your dad. Guess where I am? High above the white clouds in a silver airplane . . . going to the Caribbean via Florida for the summer. How about that? No swimming with the ducks . . . but, whoa, I'll have to ask Roger about sharks.

You remember I told you about my sister Madalyn's friend Roger? The one who taught her all the psychic stuff? He came back to Seattle a few weeks ago and rescued my brother from his wicked foster parents. I think of Roger as King Arthur and Merlin rolled into one.

Then he whisked me away from Aunt Linda. Well, for part of the summer anyway. She wasn't going to let me go. Said she had always thought she'd take me down the Oregon coast on her vacation. That stunned me. I'd always thought I was a bother to her.

Aunt Linda, Roger, Phillip, and I were having dinner together while this discussion was going on. Before I could start pleading and crying that I wanted to be with my twin, Roger gave me a look. When he'd finished eating, he pushed back his chair, dabbed his silky black mustache with his napkin, and told Aunt Linda she makes the best meals he'd ever eaten. "And," he said, "why don't you spend your vacation with us in the Caribbean? There's a delightful little restaurant where we stay that I think you'd enjoy."

And big old Aunt Linda just melted.

Opps, have to clear my tray now because I can see the flight attendants wheeling the lunch cart down the aisle. Seems like they just served us orange juice and honeyed peanuts. I'm not complaining!

Ain't life without Gessert great? Wonder who'll be the social studies teacher next year?

See you in September,
Faith

168

ABOUT THE AUTHORS

Barthe DeClements says, "Although I have a traditional Master's Degree in educational psychology, I have, like my son Christopher, been exploring nontraditional methods of expanding awareness for the past seventeen years. *Double Trouble* is an attempt to share some of these explorations with young people."

Christopher Greimes says, "I have thrived on hopping freight trains, felling gigantic timber in the Olympic Rain Forest, and performing in a rock and roll band.

"This quest for adventure has led me into new worlds. Through my characters, readers have an opportunity to experience some of the realities I've encountered."

Barthe DeClements is the author of the best-selling *Nothing's Fair in Fifth Grade*, *Sixth Grade Can Really Kill You*, *How Do You Lose Those Ninth Grade Blues?*, *Seventeen and In-between*, and *I Never Asked You To Understand Me*. She lives near Snohomish, Washington. Her son, Christopher Greimes, lives nearby. This is his first book.